Different Shades of Gray
By Sable Jordan

Chapter 1

Do me a favor.

Four little innocent words are what got me here, stuck in a house with nineteen other gaggling girls, all of them presently screaming and fawning over the arrival of one Jacob Logan—sexy bachelor, multi-millionaire, and the media's favorite bad boy.

Wait. I'm getting ahead of myself. Let me slow down. Before you catch up with where I am now, you need to know the back-story.

A month ago Charlene called, begging me to perform the aforementioned favor, and hold her place in line for the über-popular reality show *Free Money*. She was flying in from a photo shoot in Jamaica and didn't want to be last when she got to the audition. No problem.

I'd only seen the show once during the previous season and decided it wouldn't make my list of allotted television viewing. I'm more of a History/ Discovery/ NatGeo kind of girl. Reality TV isn't really my thing. And that's probably because on the one episode I happened to have time to watch I saw things no human being should witness on television without a subscription to the Spice Channel. I mean, sure it's a God-given talent to slide from the top of a pole and drop into the splits on the floor and still manage to have all your lady bits in tact, but did I really need to see that?

So anyhow, there I stood, awaiting the arrival of my jet-setting model sister so she could have her chance to be one of the twenty ladies chosen to fight, bitch, spit, scream, and scratch out their displays of affection for a total stranger—on national television.

Love. Ain't it grand?

I'd been there two hours already, flipping through Dr. Samuel Shem's uproariously funny and frighteningly realistic novel *The House of God*, as the hundreds of other girls preened for the outdoor cameras that were shooting footage for the behind-the-scenes portion of the show. One girl actually showed her bare breasts! What was Charlene getting herself into? I didn't have time to fully process that thought when my cell phone played out the familiar Danity Kane song *Bad Girl* that was my custom ringtone for Char.

"Where are you?" I asked, noticing I had moved ominously close to the red doors that girls went into but didn't come out of.

"You'll never believe this. The plane had to land in Phoenix first for a minor repair and then, when we finally got to LA, Tyler's Beemer had a flat. The tow truck driver is fixing it now so we should get to Hollywood in no time."

Ahh yes. Tyler. Char's "agent" and on-again-off-again boyfriend. Six feet four inches of lean, hot, steamy man-cake, as Char would say. I on the other hand think he's a completely vile and insufferable jackass, and have utilized every opportunity to tell her so. Char may think he's dreamy, but I know him to be a disgusting, lying cheat, and the good Lord himself couldn't convince me otherwise. The knowledge that he was within a fifty-mile radius of my present location made my skin crawl. Then it dawned on me that he must have been the one who put this harebrained scheme into Char's beautiful, if currently empty, head.

"Tow truck driver. Of course. I'd hate for *le petit jackass* to damage his manicure," I mocked, dropping in and out of a horrible French accent.

"Come on, sweets. Don't give me grief. I've had a rough day as it is. I know if you were here we'd have been gone hours ago."

Hours?

I heard the jackass mumble something in the background I couldn't make out, but no doubt he'd just noticed her flub.

"How long have you been in LA, Char?" I asked suspiciously, hearing the lie form in her head.

"Umm…Less than an hour."

"Chaaaar."

She sighed. "Okay, we got in at six this morning."

"What?" I screamed loud enough that everyone turned to look at me, but I didn't care one iota. I glanced at my watch. "You gotta be shittin' me! It's one in the afternoon and I've been standing in this freakin' line for two hours for you so *you* could get on this stupid show. I'm literally minutes from being in front of the casting director, and you tell me *now* that you've been here for the last seven hours?"

"Well, me and Tyler had some making up to do. We got into this really huge fight in Jamaica because—"

"Couldn't care less, Char. You knew I was coming here after a ten-hour shift and you pull this? I'm outta here."

"Wait!" she screamed then went on in a rush, "please, please, please don't leave. I need you to appear before the casting director for me. Tyler says if I can get on this show it could really be the break my career needs."

Hmm. So this is what the truth looks like.

"Oh, then let me just drop everything and work on *your* problem? You should have been here, Charlene." I started inching from the line when she dropped the bomb—the one she knows I can never say "no" to.

"But mom would want you to help me. Please," she whined.

I waited for a full minute before I answered. I mean, sure our mom would want us to help each other no matter what, but honestly, how long could I let her get away with this excuse?

"Number eighty-six fifty-three. That's eight. Six. Five. Three," the production assistant yelled out into the crowd before answering a question from one of the gophers who had returned with yet another round of Starbucks.

I looked down at the numbered yellow page in my hand, which, to my horror, was the same number that had just been called. I stared at the gray Nikes on my feet, the horribly faded blue jeans on my legs, and the less-than-trendy tee shirt with the saying "1f u c4n r34d 7h1s u r34lly n33d 70 g37 l41d" emblazoned across my chest.

It dawned on me that I could read the shirt upside down.

"Eight, six, five, three," the assistant yelled again.

"Please," Char whined.

"Gotta go," I grumbled, disconnecting the call and turning off my phone. Let her suffer.

Gathering all my courage, and the dingy green backpack I toted through life, I waltzed through the red doors, if for no other reason than to see where everyone came out on the other side.

* * * *

{12:55pm}

Jacob Logan was running late. Which was entirely normal when it came to things he didn't want to do. And right now, he couldn't think of anything he wanted to do less than this.

Three months ago his parents managed to do what all parents did and meddled in his personal life. In response his rebellious side—which he tried really hard to suppress—had gotten the best of him and led him to accept his aunt Jorja's offer of doing a reality show.

At the time the idea seemed heaven-sent. He had some free time from his demanding work life and being the only man in a house with twenty beautiful women would be a welcome change of pace. But things started moving very fast with production of this show, and to take his mind off of what he couldn't control he started working even harder than normal.

Fourteen hours ago he was in Tokyo closing the deal on a new hotel, opening his new nightclub, *Koodori Doragon*—the Dancing Dragon—and letting the paparazzi snap the photos that would no doubt appear on all the blogs and in the glossies over the next few days. No such thing as bad publicity, right?

He hopped a jet from Tokyo, drafting proposals during the eleven-hour flight so he could be in L.A. for the last casting for the show. He arrived only an hour ago, giving him very little time to shower and dress before rushing to the club where the casting was being held.

He phoned Jorja—or "AJ" as he called her—who was also the producer, when his Range Rover pulled up to the club, and was told to come in once the next girl exited.

And there she was, feet jammed into high-heels, breasts spilling out of the slit in her brand new "vintage" top, and super-tight jeans that made her mid section bulge out over the band. She had a shoulder bag that was too bright and too big, and her long hair was tangled in the mass of accessories that hung on her neck and wrists. He wasn't even about to comment about the face paint.

"Oh, well isn't that sexy," he said caustically. "Why am I doing this again, Marcus?"

"Because you're a masochist," his buddy laughed. "You could have just settled down with that nice girl your parents decided you should marry."

Jake groaned thinking about the woman his parents told him would be "a perfect wife" for him. Simone was a beautiful woman, true enough, with a pleasant disposition. But she was dumb as a box of rocks. On the few dates they'd gone on Jake tried to get her opinion on current events—from the presidential election to stem cell research to the flavor of the Tandoori chicken they were eating—and he found that she took whatever position he had on an issue. He even started an argument just to see how she'd respond and got more of her smiling and nodding.

"That's the problem. Simone was *too* nice. The kind of nice that never shows emotion, never let's you know when she's mad, never forms an opinion. Always smiling and giggling and agreeing with you. Then when you least expect it, bam! She's stabbing you in the neck with a fork while you're sleeping." He grimaced and rubbed his throat. "Besides, my parents have no right to try to arrange a marriage for me, and especially not with some Stepford wife. What century is this?"

"So you do the polar opposite and go on a reality show to find true love? The fork may have been less painful than this, my man," Marcus chuckled. "You can't really blame them for wantin' to see you happy. You should've let AJ pick the girls for you, though. The guy from last season had a nice group."

"To your first question who said I was looking for love, true or otherwise? But if I were I sincerely doubt I'd find it on this show. And to the second, I missed all the other castings and watching the tapes doesn't really give you a great feel of the person you're dealing with. You know I like to do all my business deals face-to-face. You comin' in?"

Marcus shook his head. "Nope. Gotta meet the crew at Vic's Cameras to pick up our gear. Besides, I lack the social filter that stops most people from laughing at train wrecks like that last girl. And I want to be surprised when I come to visit you at the mansion."

They both laughed before Marcus asked, "So since it's not for love, and we know it's not for publicity, why are you doing the show? "

That was the very question Jake had been asking himself. Why *was* he doing the show? As Marcus pointed out, he didn't need the publicity. He had hotels and nightclubs worldwide, and the media loved to delve into his personal life, no matter how nonexistent it currently was. He certainly wasn't looking for a serious relationship; been there, don't that, bought a shirt, and no plans to visit any time soon.

Spite? Maybe. A way to prove to his parents they couldn't keep meddling in his personal affairs. But he knew deep down it wouldn't help a bit. They were parents. They'd jump in uninvited whenever they wanted. It was their job.

Was it for fun? A diversion from the vigorous pace he'd set for his life? Maybe just to get over... The more he thought about it the more he didn't know. But he wouldn't find out sitting in the truck. He opened the door and got out, then turned back to his friend and shrugged, "Because I'm a masochist."

Hurrying through the green doors, he found AJ sitting in the small dark room, smoking her usual cigarette, a tray overflowing with filters and ashes just within reach. Thankfully a window was open somewhere.

"You're late," she said in a gravelly voice. "Thought you weren't comin' at all, nephew."

"I can't say I wasn't having second thoughts," he admitted, giving her a quick hug before taking his seat and folding his long legs beneath the table. Sitting in the truck he had seriously considered backing out of the show entirely, but decided against mentioning it to AJ. If today didn't go well he'd cancel and help her find a replacement. "How's this been goin'? You look exhausted."

"Six castings across the country and if you've seen one girl, you've seen 'em all. And they've all got the same story; model or actress, extravagant clothes they can't afford to make up for in style what they lack in personality; all singing 'Some day my prince will come' in their heads with dollar signs in their eyes. Half of them have been sent here by some scumbag agent who's telling them this will be their stepping-stone to stardom. The rest actually believe they can fall in love with you in a couple months." She took a drag of her cigarette and went into a coughing fit. "You're the poor bastard I feel sorry for. A few days in that house and you'll be slippin' arsenic into your Glenlivet."

Jake chuckled, twisting the top off a bottle of water that was on the table. "You mean you don't believe in all that fairytale crap? I didn't think they'd let someone so cynical produce a show about love."

"Fairytales are for little girls with pigtails and lollipops. My hair's too short and I prefer Marlboros."

"You're really making me want to do this less and less, AJ," he smiled sardonically.

Jorja laughed, coughed, and laughed again. "Hey, my job is to find you twenty girls who are attractive, borderline obnoxious, and willing to put on a good show. The fairytale has been conspicuously left out of the contract. Honey, if that's what you're looking for," she paused as she stubbed out her cigarette, pulled another from the pack, stuck it between her lips and lit it, taking a slow drag, "we might as well start casting for next season."

* * * *

{1:10 pm}

The red doors concealed a small brick-walled room that looked like it functioned as some bohemian poetry club when not being used to sift through the tons of people dying to become reality stars. Opposite the red doors I entered were a set of army green doors—so *that's* where everyone goes. The faint smell of stale cigarettes lingered in the cool air. There was a raised platform where a bar stool sat with a bright light aimed in the general area. I was ushered in by the production assistant, asked to sit on the stool, told to hold up my number, and then the brightest flash in the world nearly blinded me. Don't you get to commit a crime in exchange for a mugshot? 'Cause I'm killing Char for this.

"Your name?" a raspy female voice asked from the darkness beyond. She had all the enthusiasm of someone having a root canal sans anesthetic.

Once my eyes adjusted to the light, I could make out the outline of a person who appeared to be female, the solid form of a male figure, and a video camera.

"Charlo-*ene. Charlene* Roberts."

"Age?"

"Twenty-eight." At least that wasn't a lie.

"A little old to be on this show, don'tcha think," she stated, then she coughed up what sounded like her left lung before inhaling smoke from her cigarette, the red ember on the end glowing brightly before being swallowed up by the surrounding darkness again.

"Oh, yeah, I'm the epitome of decrepitude," I said sarcastically. "Besides, Logan's thirty-three. What would he want with some pop tart when he can have a real woman?" That last response rolled off my tongue like I actually meant it. This might not be so hard after all.

Raspy choked out a laugh. "So, what is it you do for a living?"

"I'm a doc—er—model. I model."

The man in the room snorted. Must've heard that one before.

"You aren't dressed like you're remotely fashion-conscious much less a model."

I couldn't argue with her there, but managed to improvise. "Oh, but this is my lucky shirt," I enthused. "It's got personality, like me. I have a Gucci dress, but not a *lucky* Gucci dress."

"And you've got moxie. I like that," she chuckled then returned to her cigarette. "So, Char-*lene*, why do you want to be on *Free Money*?"

I got stumped there because I didn't. Quite frankly, I thought the show was everything wrong with the current horrible state of most relationships. Men thought they should have a multitude of women at their beck-and-call, and women thought they had to compete to get a man whose attention was fickle at best. Madness. All of it.

Personal opinions aside, I fished around in my head for a prefect response, and a bit of Angelina Jolie acting prowess. "Because I think once I got to know him, maybe I could give my heart to Jacob Logan."

I'd have batted my eyelashes but that might have been overkill.

The room was quiet for a moment, except for Raspy inhaling her cigarette and coughing.

"I can't help but notice your eyes, Charlene. They're very pretty. Are they contacts?" Raspy asked.

"No, this is the natural color." I get this question a lot, so I'm used to it. I guess some people haven't seen a woman with milk chocolate skin and naturally light gray eyes, although it's not so uncommon for me. I see two daily. "It's a Roberts family trait. Most of the women on my father's side have gray eyes." I leaned forward on the stool and let the light catch my peepers to make them glow, deciding to take advantage of my audience's full attention.

"The story goes that when one of the small groups of early Scandinavian explorers got to America, one of the men met the princess of the Abenaki tribe of present-day New England. He thought she was beautiful; reddish-brown skin, dark eyes and lustrous jet-black hair, and he fell in love with her immediately. She on the other hand thought he was a giant of a man, with skin pale as a ghost and gray eyes perfect for haunting. Nonetheless, they became friends and eventually she began to love him as well.

"But their whirlwind romance was short-lived because he was going back across the seas, unsure if he'd ever return. So he asked her father the chief for her hand in marriage. The chief wanted his only daughter to be happy, but couldn't bear the thought of losing her to some mysterious land far away. So he devised a challenge, one he was certain could never be met, and told the Norseman he could marry the princess if he could give her his eyes."

I paused for dramatic effect; after all, as kids I'd told this story hundreds of times to Charlene to get her to fall asleep, and I knew how to stoke the flames.

On cue Raspy asked, "So what happened?"

"Well, when he told the princess what her father proposed, he grabbed the dagger from his waistband and raised it to his left eye, fully prepared to gouge it out, for if Odin, the one-eyed Norse god, could surrender his eye for a drink in the Well of Wisdom, surely the Norseman could give his own eyes for true love.

"But the princess stilled his hand, took the dagger, and cut a length of his sandy blonde hair instead. Then she cut a short piece of her own hair, mixed them with his, and separated them into two piles. Finally she took long stalks of sweet grass and, as was custom, joined them with the locks, weaving two rings.

"The Norseman watched in silence as her slender fingers worked, and when she was done she put the rings between them, grasping both of his hands. He looked at her sadly, wishing there was some way he could change their fate.

"'I would gladly give you my eyes,' he told her. 'I know, but then you could not see your way home and back to me, my love,' she replied. 'So we will be married anyway.' She spoke a few words over the rings then bowed to gently kiss his hands, and he did the same. Then each slipped a ring onto the other's hand and she said, 'Kassiwi pazego.'

"'Kassiwi pazego,' he replied, and with that they shared a kiss and were married. The explorers left the next day, and the chief was pleased to still have his daughter."

The room was dead silent when I finished that part of the legend—even Raspy had put out her cigarette—but I knew they would want to hear the full story, because every time I got to this part Char would wake up, wanting to hear the end.

Everyone always wants to hear how it ends.

This time the gentleman spoke. "Did they ever see each other again?" His voice was warm and deep like chocolate poured slowly over caramel, and it took me a moment to regain my train of thought as I was pointlessly trying to make out his face in a sea of black.

I gave up and nodded, continuing in the whimsical voice all fairytales must be told. "Yes, they did… many years later. When the Norseman returned to the village he saw the princess, older but still just as beautiful as the day he married her. He did not let her know he had returned going instead straight to the cabin of the chief, determined this time to get the old man's blessing so his secret wife could have a proper marriage.

"When he was granted an audience he said, 'I am Igrár, of the Norse. I have returned, Sougmou, for your daughter's hand in marriage.'

"The chief sent an aide to fetch his daughter, and when she arrived her dark eyes were bright with unshed tears. She was so happy her husband had returned. The chief looked at his daughter but his face remained cold as he addressed the Norseman. He said to Igrár, 'My daughter told me you are kassiwi pazego.' The Norseman was shocked, wondering why the princess would tell her father of their secret marriage. Surely he'd never allow it now. Then the chief smiled broadly and said, 'It is lucky for you that you passed the test.'

"Igrár sighed, "You are wrong, Sougmou, for as you can see I still have my eyes. How could anyone meet such a challenge?' The chief motioned to the door where someone entered the cabin, and when Igrár turned he finally understood. Standing next to the princess was a beautiful young girl with long black hair, reddish-brown skin, and his own gray eyes." I paused with the ending, letting it all sink in as I leaned back on the stool and shrugged. "They've been in the family ever since."

After a few moments Raspy sparked another cigarette then coughed out, "So that's the story of how you got your eyes?"

"And my keen ability to build furniture," I assured. "I'm a whiz with an entertainment center."

They both laughed.

"Thank you, Charlene. We'll contact you if you're a finalist."

I gathered my bag and headed for the green doors. As I turned the knob the man said, "Wait! What does kassiwi pazego mean?"

I smiled brightly and responded into the darkness, "Together we're one."

Chapter 2

Three weeks had passed and I hadn't heard anything from the producers of *Free Money*, not that I was looking for it, mind you. I had plenty of other things on my plate, like my last rotation of residency. After today's shift at Kaiser I'd be a full-blown doctor. Not *resident* Doctor Roberts... just Doctor Roberts, fully licensed physician. With a real shift, and finally a real paycheck! And it couldn't have happened fast enough. I'd wanted to be a doctor since I can remember, just like our father, Charles Roberts IV. As you can imagine, that's where Char and I get our names. In our family there's always been a male heir to carry the name Charles Roberts, until Char and I were born. There'd be no Charles Roberts V. So our mother, genius that she was, decided to name us both after him.

Our father died in a car accident when we were about ten. He was leaving the hospital one afternoon after a long surgery when a drunk driver slammed into his car, killing him instantly. So we were very close with our mother Kimberly, who made sure we knew and remembered everything about him. Born under the sign of Gemini, she said he had two distinct sides—one the hard working, serious neurosurgeon and the other a carefree lover of the world and everything in it.

I remember when I was twelve I told my mom I wanted to be a doctor, and she smiled with a knowing glint in her eyes, saying, "Of course you do. Why else do you think you were named Charlotte?" Then Char said, "But there's alotta stuff I wanna do. Do I gotta choose one?" And my mom kissed her on her head saying, "You can do all of them if you want, because you're Charlene. And both of you are two wholes to a whole."

I didn't understand that at the time, but I get it now. *Two wholes to a whole.* Each of us our own person, yet in some way we were both our father. He was a great dad, and for a man with two different sides—one black, one white, so to speak—mom was his shade of gray. She was his balance, his kindred; the one person in the world who truly completed him. And mom was single-handedly the sweetest person I've ever known. I'm not just saying that because she's my mom (although there may be a slight bias). She always told us to never give up on what was important, and pushed us to go after our dreams. Well, here I am a shift away from reaching mine, and it's really hard having gotten her without her.

Kimberly Roberts, my mom—*our* mom—best mom in the world, lost her short battle with cancer nine months ago.

The residency program is intense so there wasn't much opportunity for me to sit with her while she was sick, although I checked in on her every shift. I still regret that I wasn't there for her more often, and I told her that the last time I saw her. Even on the day she died she told us, "I don't have any regrets. I'm so proud of you both, and whatever you do, stick together and you'll reach your dreams."

I'm getting misty-eyed just thinking about her.

And leave it to Char's copious coughing to intrude on my reverie.

"Can you bring me some soup, Charlie?" she whined. I hate it when my sister's sick. For some reason she thinks she needs to be waited on, but it's a fatigue cold. She'd been working too hard, not eating properly, and her immune system was making her pay for not slowing down.

"Sure, Char." I really need to learn how to tell this girl no. "But you're not gonna die if you get up and get it yourself. In fact, you'll probably feel better if you move around a bit. You don't have a fever and the cough is mild."

"It feels like the swine flu," she pouted.

"It's *not* the swine flu, Char. You're being ridiculous. It's a mild case of fatigue. I'm sure you'll live, but if you don't dibs on your television," I joked, going into the kitchen in our condo and making her soup. When I got back—soup, crackers, and orange juice in tow—Char hung up her cell phone and turned to me, her smile as big as the Cheshire cat's.

"OMG!" she screamed, bouncing on the bed. "I didn't think you could do it, but you did it!"

I stared at her blankly for a moment as she rummaged through her bedside drawer and fished out an old copy of *US Weekly*. She flipped the magazine open and creased it down the center then placed it on her bed before me, taking the tray of food and settling it over her lap.

"Did what?" I picked it up and stared down at the page featuring a shot of Jacob Logan, the headline screaming STARLET DROPS BAD BOY! The thing had to be over a year old, but the page was as crisp as if it had been purchased yesterday.

"*Free Money* wants me on the show!"

I'm dumb-founded for a moment. Technically, they want *me* on the show, but that's not what's needling me. Why didn't she think I could do it? I know she's the model and I'm the do-it-yourself tomboy, but jeez, give a girl some credit. Play up to the camera, smile, and be mysterious enough that they want to know what's behind the grin. It's arithmetic, not quantum physics.

"When do you go on," I continued, deciding against voicing what's going on in my head.

She dug into her soup with zest, no trace of the dreaded swine flu that rendered her weak and whiny only moments before.

"Well, they start taping on Wednesday right here at a mansion in LA, somewhere near the beach I think. Which is perfect, 'cause I have a shoot in Costa Rica on Monday. But I'll be back Tuesday. Oh, Charlie! It's really happening!"

I stole a cracker from her plate and popped it into my mouth.

"One reality show won't make you a star, Char. Hey! That rhymes!" I giggled as she frowned at my corny joke. "Just don't get too worked up yet."

"Still," she said wistfully, "even if it doesn't make my career, Jake Logan is *oh* so sexy. Just look at those brown eyes. And that smile. And those lips! Mmmm! Super kissable."

I glanced at the page. True enough Jake is fine. Mahogany skin, dark brown eyes, and those lips do look "super kissable". But everything about him screams player and that makes him not my type. I only remember a little about the whole fiasco between Jacob Logan and his ex. Apparently he'd been cheating on her. I've been that route already with the cheating boyfriend, and why anyone would sign up to date a known cheater is beyond me, but who am I to squash a dream?

"When do you leave for Costa Rica?"

"Tomorrow morning, so I'm gonna stay at Tyler's tonight."

I shook my head and smiled sardonically. "But you have swine flu, remember? And two seconds ago you were all gaga for Jake. Besides, I don't know what you see in Tyler. He's a worthless piece of—"

"Charlotte! Can we not do this again? I'm not in love with him. He's my friend... with occasional benefits," she smiled, crunching down on a cracker. "Plus he's doing pretty good at getting me shoots that can further my career. So let it go, okay?"

"And how many other girls do you think he's promising the moon to, Char?"

"I don't know," she mumbled between spoonfuls of broth, trying to keep the hurt expression from her face. "We're not exclusive, so he can do whatever, or *whoever*, he wants."

I fixed her with my serious stare, knowing she was lying. "But you want more, don't you?"

She didn't respond.

"Whatever. I gotta go." I dropped the magazine on her bed and turned to leave.

"Where are you going? It's ten-thirty at night."

"It's the last shift of the last day of my last rotation. Tomorrow morning, I'll officially be Charlotte Roberts, M.D.," I beamed, striking a Charlie's Angels pose and saying my name like it belonged to a super-spy instead of a mild-mannered physician.

Char cocked her head like this was the first time she'd ever heard I wanted to be a doctor, let alone a shift away from completing the task.

"Congratulations," she said around another mouthful of soup. "Guess things are finally looking up for both of us!"

* * * *

My last shift in the emergency room before a much needed—if forced—vacation. Since I didn't take any time off when mom passed, the head honchos decided once I was done with my residency I'd go on leave. I wanted to protest, but now I'm glad I hadn't. I could really use the break.

It's a bit hectic here at first, but once you get the hang of it you're golden. Tonight though was beyond crazy. I had three unrelated cases of pneumonia caused by the same bacteria. Another patient was painting his living room around four this afternoon when the ladder buckled, causing him to fall off the side and hit his head on the floor. When the headache continued and his eyesight started blurring, he called a neighbor to bring him into the ER. Turns out he hit so hard he fractured a bone in his skull and the headache and blurry eyesight were due to his brain swelling. The specialist was able to reduce the edema and his vision should return to normal, but any longer and the results could have been tragic.

Still another patient, a cute thirteen-year-old girl named Erica, had dislocated her shoulder and shattered her forearm doing stunts on her skateboard to impress some boy named Jimmy who she thinks is the bees knees. She's really excited he told her he'd sign her cast. The things we women do for love.

Anyhow, these were just some of the major incidents. I also had your run-of-the-mill stomachaches, rashes, colds, and cuts to tend to. Why I decided to be an ER doc I'll never know.

The girl they've just brought in is a twenty-three-year-old college student named Amanda Sullivan. Amanda was out drinking with her friends and someone may have slipped something into her drink. She wasn't responding when the EMTs got to her, and they'd been performing CPR on her for a while before they got a heartbeat. Back on this side of the light, her vitals were faint, until about forty seconds ago when Amanda went into a seizure—and then they were off the charts.

Being that she was on a bed with equipment rooted to her when the seizure started, there was a serious risk that she'd pull something down and hurt herself as her arms and legs flailed about then locked her whole body into a rigid spasm. She got through it without incident and we rolled her on her side just in time for the post-seizure heaving to begin.

"Get a sample of this over to Tox!" I called to a nurse passing by, shoving the yellow tray and its contents into his hands. "Amanda? Amanda, can you hear me?"

Her blue eyes fluttered open, she made eye contact, and then they closed again. The steady beeping of the monitors indicated the episode had passed, so we carefully rolled her onto her back and elevated her legs slightly.

With a couple nurses nearby I left the curtained cubicle to talk with the EMTs.

"Any indication she has a history of seizures?"

Scott, the lead member of the team, started rattling off the details. "I just went out to ask her friends, but they didn't know. Apparently they had gone out for a drink to celebrate someone's birthday. They ended up in a bar and some guy kept hitting on Amanda. She finally accepted a drink from the guy, Jack and Coke, but she only had a few swallows because she told her friends it tasted funny. Her friends went off to dance, Amanda stayed at the table. When they turned around the guy was trying to drag her off the barstool, but one of the girls saw him and he took off. Her friends tried talking to her, but Amanda wasn't responding so they called 911 thinking she might have been drugged. Her parents are on their way, but I think they live up in the Bay Area. Could be a couple hours before they get here."

"Whew! Well all we can do is give her fluids and watch her until the tox-report comes back. I don't want to administer anything that may cause another episode. Thanks guys."

The other EMTs went back to the van to restock and check equipment. But Scott, as he'd done for the last four months, followed me to the cafeteria for my break.

"So I hear it's your last day of residency."

"Yep! Then a two month vacation before I start working here full time."

"Whoa, I won't see you here for two whole months?" he asked, looking truly disappointed. "Then you have to let me take you out and celebrate. My treat."

Scott was a muscular six-foot-three with incredibly soft brown eyes and dark hair and was completely adorable in that 'little brother' kind of way that made you want to pinch his cheeks, ruffle his hair, and make him a peanut butter and jelly sandwich. But he had the persistence of the twenty-nine-year-old man he was—the one who wouldn't take no for an answer.

"When will you get over this Jungle Fever thing you've got for me, Scotty?" I asked with a grin as I waited for the vending machine to finish dispensing my drink. I slid open the safety glass and removed the Styrofoam cup, setting it on the counter to prep my sixth cup of coffee for the night. In truth I despise the stuff, but it's part and parcel of the position, kind of like cops and doughnuts.

"Come on, Charlie. Don't shoot me down again. What does a man have to do to get a date with you?"

"Flatline." A little ER humor. "Honestly, I don't date people I work with, and aren't you and Nancy supposed to be going out?" I asked, reminding him of the nurse's aide who was hell-bent on getting her some Scott.

"Argh! Don't mention that name to me ever again! We went out on *one* date—one date! And that was about a month ago. She shows up at my apartment for two weeks straight trying to go out again! The woman's certifiable!"

"Because she wants a relationship and not just a one-night stand?"

Scott rolled his eyes.

"You did sleep with her, right?" I continued, taking a sip of the hot coffee and swallowing hard like it was whiskey instead of java. I can't wait to get on a normal shift so I don't need this stuff anymore. "And it was more than one date. Well, that's what she said anyway."

Scott raised an inquisitive eyebrow then grinned, leaning against the machine and into my personal space. "I think your gray eyes are turning green, Charlie. Jealousy is sexy on you. But anything is sexy on you."

"That's Doctor Charlie to you, bub," I said, hitting him playfully on the arm. "And whatever you and Nancy do in your bedroom is your own business. Although her recounts of the encounter were quite descriptive."

"Well, *Doctor* Charlie, you don't have to get the info second-hand if you want to know about my bedroom expertise. I'm more than willing to give you a first-hand account," he said silkily, staring me straight in the eyes.

"Did you miss sexual harassment training?"

"Both times."

I shook my head and chuckled. "You're impossible."

"Scott!" a voice shrieked across the empty cafeteria. "They told me you were here. Why haven't you called me back?" Nancy asked, making a beeline across the room toward us.

Scott's face dropped as he saw the woman approach.

"I take it she doesn't know the affair is over?" I murmured.

"Come on, Charlie. Dinner," he pleaded quickly, risking life and limb and an angry Nancy to get this date.

"Sorry sweetie, I love you too much as a friend to ruin that. Now get out of here before Nancy rips you a new one," I teased. "Proctology is not a specialty I want to go into, although you do have a cute butt."

Scott smiled crookedly, hugged me briefly, and ran out like his cute ass was on fire.

"Nancy," I said, stopping the girl in her pursuit. "Could you do me a favor and check to be sure the tox-report is on rush for Amanda, the patient who just came in?"

Nancy paused near me running a hand through her short dark tresses, torn between going after Scott and doing what the ER doc asked her. "Sure, Charlie. But can I ask you something? Why do you think Scott won't talk to me? I mean, I see you two talking all the time, and, well... does he ever mention me?"

Poor kid. "Nancy, Scott's a nice guy—but he's a guy. I don't think he's ready to give you the kind of relationship you're looking for."

She frowned as we walked to the elevators to get back to the ER. "Relationship? He's cute, and the sex is good and all, don't get me wrong, but I don't want a relationship."

It was my turn to frown. "Then why have you been hounding him to call you?"

The elevator arrived and the doors slid open revealing an empty carriage. We stepped inside and the doors glided shut. Nancy pressed the button then turned to me, looking as though I were the newest idiot on the block. "I left my iPod in his car the other day and I want it back. Damn thing cost me three hundred bucks!"

Chapter 3

"Charlie," Nancy called, walking briskly into the ER. I was leaving a patient who had taken to saying, "What's up, Doc?" in his best Bugs Bunny voice. Because I haven't heard *that* a million times already. He was the last patient of this last shift, and damn if I wasn't glad to be getting out of here. Two months of me working on my pride and joy—a '62 Harley Davidson DuoGlide, a project mom and I started a few months before she was diagnosed. For obvious reasons we never got to finish. But with Char gone off to some mansion in who-cares-where, I'll be all by my onesies! Yes!

I turned to see where Nancy had called for me, my gaze dropping to the papers in her hand. "Tox-report?"

"Yep, just as you're going out the door, right? Leave it to Tox to take eleven hours on a rush."

I took the report from her hand and read the results. Amanda had gotten a Jack and Coke, all right. But that was 'coke' as in cocaine. Ingesting cocaine for an epileptic is just begging for an episode. And the Jack Daniel's didn't help either. Thank God she'd emptied her stomach on her own, and the saline should have helped to flush her system.

"Her parents just got here and are in the room with her now. Did you want to have Doctor Havershan take over, or are you going in?"

Vacation was calling, but a few more minutes to spare the parents the drama of dealing with a new doctor wouldn't kill me. "I'll finish and then I'm outta here. Thanks."

I trudged to the cubicle and pulled back the curtains, met with the wet eyes of Amanda's mother, and the furious glare of her father. "Hello, I'm Doctor Roberts," I said, shaking hands with both parents. "How are you feeling, Amanda?"

The girl shifted slightly, making the paper gown crinkle and her brown hair fall across her face. "Like a sledgehammer hit me," she croaked, her voice weak from retching. "My whole body hurts. I still don't know what happened."

"Well, you had a seizure and blacked out. Do you have a history of seizures?"

"She had a few as a child because of low blood pressure, but she hasn't had one since she was nine," Mrs. Sullivan answered, tenderly wiping her daughter's hair back.

That explained a lot.

"Do you remember anything from tonight?" I asked Amanda.

She nodded slightly. "Just going out with my friends. We went to a bar in Hollywood, *The Flame*. We had a few drinks and then it all went black."

"Unfortunately, someone put something in your drink. Cocaine to be exact."

Mrs. Sullivan gasped; Mr. Sullivan cursed. Normal responses for any parent in their situation. Then they both started talking simultaneously. Mrs. Sullivan admonishing her daughter for having a social life and Mr. Sullivan asking "Why in the hell aren't the cops out there looking for the bastard that did this to my little girl?"

"I'll have an officer come in and get your statement in a minute. The good news is that your last blood sample was clean.When you took the drink, the combination of alcohol and the narcotic probably caused your blood pressure to drop really quickly triggering the first episode at the bar. The need to vomit triggered the second episode here. We'll hold you for a few more hours, just to monitor your vitals, and if all is well you're free to go."

Amanda smiled brightly. "I'm feeling better already."

"Just take it easy for the next week or so. Don't do anything that's stressful. In fact, bed rest for a few days at least. And no alcohol."

Her bright smile fell flat instantly. "I had something planned in a few days, but it shouldn't be too rough."

Amanda's father broke in, his face turning red. "Oh no! You're not doin' a darn thing. Tell her, doc."

I was getting to it, sheesh! "Amanda I'd prefer if you did absolutely nothing, but there's really no reason you can't go out so long as you keep it light, okay? No skydiving or bungee-jumping."

She shook her head fiercely, a reassuring look on her face. "Don't worry, doc. Nothing nearly as stressful as that."

* * * *

By the time I got home from my shift the next morning, Char was gone and she'd taken her swine flu with her. I took a hot shower, poured a cup of Chamomile tea, turned on the television, and promptly fell into a slumber so deep anything deeper would have rendered me clinically dead. By the time I peeled my face from my pillow nine hours later I had three messages from a hoarse Char checking to see that I was okay and to let me know that she'd arrived in Costa Rica.

Let the vacation officially begin!

It was nine o'clock Sunday night, which made it eleven where Char was. I picked up my cell and called her, noticing I'd just missed an interesting piece on the Science Channel. I flipped through the channels for something to watch and came across a marathon of last season's *Free Money*. Why not? A couple days of mind-numbing television wouldn't hurt.

The basis of the show was that one rich bachelor *possibly*—though highly unlikely—looking for "love" was put in a house with twenty women who would compete for his affections over the course of two months through a series of challenges to win special dates with him. After each date there was an elimination ceremony and one of the women would be sent home. The last woman standing wins. How's that for civilized behavior?

Last season's bachelor was actor/playboy Damian Royce. Notorious for flaunting his extensive wealth and breaking hearts, Royce was presently escorting two of his ladies from the helipad at a vineyard in Sonoma, each girl clinging to an arm and looking genuinely pleased to be with him. Meanwhile, back at the mansion, girls were yelling at each other, getting into one another's faces, cursing and throwing alcohol at each other. And that's what happens in a house where too many different personalities are competing over one trophy. Oh well, Char's problem, not mine. Seven distorted international rings later she answered the phone.

"Charlie? I was gonna call you in the morning."

"Sorry. Were you sleeping? You sound terrible."

"I haven't been able to sleep much," she croaked. "My throat really hurts and I think I'm getting a fever."

"Dammit, Char, you're burned out. Fatigue stresses your immune system and makes you more easily susceptible to other immune diseases. You should have cancelled the shoot."

"Are you crazy? You don't cancel a *Broussard* photo shoot, especially not when that shoot is for Dolce and Gabbana. I would have been here if the sky were falling!"

If the sky were falling neither Dolce nor Gabbana would give two thin dimes about a photo shoot, but whatever.

"Well, at least try to get some rest. I would hate for you to be sick *and* tired in the morning."

There was a long pause on the line and I got the familiar feeling something was terribly wrong.

"What's the matter, Char?" I asked hesitantly.

"Umm, see, the shoot was supposed to start tomorrow, but the D&G marketing reps had a scheduling conflict and can't come in 'til Tuesday, so they're pushing the shoot back. Which means I won't get out of here until Wednesday evening."

I'm waiting for the other Dolce to drop.

"Aww, Char, that's too bad. But hey, on the bright side you get an extra day in Costa Rica, right? I bet it's gorgeous there this time of year."

She was quiet again, and in my past experience when Char's quiet she's thinking of an awful plan that will involve me in some way and I already know what that plan is. Call it twin telepathy.

"No, Char."

"You don't even know what I'm gonna say, Charlie."

"Whatever it is, no."

"I need you to do me another favor."

"No, Char," I said as firmly as I could, but she just kept right on talking as though I had agreed.

"Just go to the house for a couple days and we'll switch out after the first challenge."

"No, Char," I repeated, hoping her loss of hearing was temporary.

"But it'll only be three days!"

"Can't you ask for something simple, like a million dollars or an arm or something? I'm not willing to part with my already questionable sanity."

"Please, Charlie, please! You'll be living in a mansion—"

"With nineteen girls… and cameras—"

"And Jake Logan," she cut in with all the enthusiasm in her voice that her sore throat could muster. "Now who in their right mind would pass that up?"

I watched as one of the girls on the show gave another girl a lap dance worthy of any high-end Hollywood strip club. Weren't those two fighting a couple scenes ago?

"For starters I've never claimed to be in my right mind, and I'd rather do your photo shoot than be in a house with a bunch of people crazier than me. I'm a doctor, Char. Took a legally binding oath to do no harm. The ink hasn't even dried on my license and I'd lose it in a heartbeat in a place like that."

Charlene laughed like I was the one talking crazy. "Charlie, I haven't seen you in heels in almost six years, and trying to pose in them is another matter entirely. No offense, sis, but you couldn't pull off being a model."

"My point *exactly*! I couldn't pull it off, yet you want me to convince the rest of America? There's no way anyone will believe I'm a model."

"I'm not asking you to pretend to be a model any more than you'd ask me to pretend to be a doctor, sweets. I'm asking you to pretend to be me."

Okay, Char's a smart girl, but her moments of absolute pristine genius were rare, and that was definitely one of them. I couldn't argue the logic because it was flawless. I could be Char if I wanted to. God knows there were many times that we'd done this before, with classes and harmless stuff. Like the time we played a trick on our neighbor, Mr. Joseph, when we were girl scouts.

Char and I were dressed in our uniforms peddling those yummy cookies they make you sell. Char went to the front door and asked Mr. Joseph if he wanted to buy a box. He agreed and went inside to get his wallet. Then I knocked on the back door and asked Mr. Joseph if he wanted to buy a box of cookies. "I told you I was just getting my wallet," he'd said. He went back inside, and Char knocked on the front door again. After a few rounds of this Mr. Joseph was furious! We finally came clean and both showed up at the back door, and his wife, who'd put us up to it in the first place, laughed so hard she cried. Eventually Mr. Joseph started laughing, too. And then they bought the rest of our cookies. Harmless.

One of the perks of being identical twins is being in two places at once. But we'd never, and I mean *never*, done the old 'bait and switch' on a guy.

I thought it over, looking for a way out of this, but couldn't find one. Physically we're almost the exact mirrors of each other; height, size, shape, skin tone, hair length and color—well hers is styled and mine... a ponytail is a style. Anyhow, unless you know us the only way to tell us apart physically is by our eyes, and it takes most people years to figure that out. Mine are a shade of gray lighter than Char's, and I have a teeny tiny beauty mark just below the left one. I'm talking really small; practically invisible it's so tiny. The differences are so nominal they're pretty much irrelevant. This could work if I wanted to do it, but I don't.

I thought about the motorcycle sitting in our garage. That was how I had planned to spend my vacation—just me and mom's Harley. But what were a few days?

Not really believing I was agreeing to do this I sighed heavily and erased all emotion from my voice. "Call me tomorrow and we'll go over the more detailed aspects of your life as a model. And you can tell me what to pack for you, although some of my clothes'll be in the bags."

Char sing-songed sweetly into the phone. "I love you, Charlie!"

"Yeah, yeah." I said, walking into the kitchen to dump my cold tea into the sink.

"I owe you one."

"Uhh-uhn. See, you'd owe me one if I picked up your dry cleaning. You owe me *seven* just for having to go through that closet of yours!"

"Thank you, Charlie." She giggled then coughed hard.

"Go to bed and feel better. Doctor's orders," I replied, rummaging through the refrigerator for something to eat. "And I love you, too."

Chapter 4
{Day 1 of Free Money}

All caught up? Good. So now you know how I got roped into this, and I can get back to telling you how horrible it is to be stuck at a house with nineteen gaggling girls all cheering as the sleek hunter green Bentley floated into the circular drive where we're standing. These heels are killing me, as I'm much more accustomed to my flat gray Nike's than to Char's three-inch Prada stilettos. This royal blue ruffled wrap-around dress, while beautiful, is a smidge too tight, low cut, and riding a mite high on my right thigh. My hair, which is thick and curly and usually worn in an unstylish ponytail has been straightened and left down and is flying in my face. And don't even get me started on this makeup. Dark eyeliner, blue eye shadow, sparkly pink lip gunk—it's a production unto itself! This is a total Charlene makeover; exactly the person they think I am. I just keep repeating the mantra *three days, three days, three days,* while I clap and scream with the rest of the ladies.

The chauffer held open the rear door, and one Jake Logan emerged clad in a pair of dark blue jeans, black loafers, a black dress shirt open at the throat, and a cream linen blazer. A pair of aviator sunglasses donning his mahogany colored face, there's a diamond stud in his left ear and a small diamond cross on a gold chain around his neck; ironic because the man is sexy as sin.

Three days.

"Ladies, welcome to the mansion," he said in his deep baritone, an easy smile on his face. "Thank you all for coming on this journey with me. Hopefully at the end of this winding road one of you ladies will have made me a very happy man. So go on inside, get settled in, and meet me by the pool in an hour for a little mixer, okay?"

We all cheered again as he got back in the car and pulled off, then it was every woman for herself as the doors to the mansion swung open revealing a large creamy marble entryway and a pair of circular staircases. Girls moved quickly up the stairs to claim their rooms, and I admit I got caught in the frenzy; hearing Char's stilettos clicking furiously up the marble staircase.

Most of the women stopped on the second floor, frantically searching for a bed to call their own. I continued up the next flight of stairs—cursing Char for her impractical choice of running shoes—and finally came to a stop at the third and topmost floor. It seemed only a few of us made the connection, and we peeked from room to room quickly.

The floor plan was huge. There was a room with closed double doors off to the left, the words "Master Suite" written in script over them. The single doors to the other four rooms were wide open, and a fifth single-door room was closed. Each room had a different color scheme. I skipped the blue room with the flowers, the pink room (gag), and the black room with the zebra print, and opted for the purple room (my favorite color) equipped with lava lamps. I should probably have chosen the pink room for Char, but she'd just have to live with it.

I snagged a bed by the window when an enthusiastic blonde came bounding into the room.

"Isn't this house awesome?" she screamed, a huge smile on her face.

"Yeah, it's really nice."

"OMG! Can you imagine meeting Jake Logan and *living* here with him for the next two months?"

I nodded and smiled. Of course I couldn't. I'm blowing this joint in three days. *Three days, three days, three days.*

"I'm Charlene," I said, extending a hand.

"Kirsten. This is so exciting. Mind if I room with you?"

If she was always this giddy Char would be pulling her hair out in a matter of minutes. "Sure!"

Two more girls came in, Tameka and Leanne, and that completed the purple room. We were going downstairs to retrieve our bags when I got the surprise of a lifetime.

"Hi," someone said, tapping me on the shoulder.

I turned to see who and my face dropped. Pulling the girl to the platform at the bottom of the stairs on the second floor, we both stared at each other for a moment to decide if our presence in the same house might be a problem. She looked much better since her hospital stay a couple days ago, which explained why I hadn't recognized her outside. Her eyes were bright, her cheeks rosy, and she wasn't wearing a paper gown.

"I thought that was you," Amanda said tensely, flipping her brown hair off her shoulder. "I mean, it's not like you have a twin sister or something, right."

I gave a nervous giggle. This could totally ruin everything. Stay calm Charlie. No worries. "Amanda, what are you doing here? You're supposed to be on bed rest," I whispered.

"Yeah, but I told you I had something planned. Well... this is it. You're not gonna make me leave, are you? I mean I really, really, really want to be here."

Great. "Do your parents know you're here?"

She nodded, but I could tell it was less than truthful. Who am I to interfere? She's twenty-three years old. She could make her own decisions.

"No, Amanda, I won't rat you out. But you have to do a favor for me."

"Anything, Dr. Roberts."

I cringed. "That's just it. See... I'm *not* Dr. Roberts, okay?"

She stared at me with those big blue eyes like I'd just spoken Klingon instead of English.

"You're not a doctor?"

I sighed, wiping a handful of tresses out of my face.

"Can you keep a secret?"

She nodded again emphatically.

"Really, Amanda. I can't have this get out at all, okay?"

She shrugged. "You're keeping mine, I'll keep yours."

"Okay, I *am* Dr. Roberts, but on this show I'm a model named Charlene Roberts. No medicine, no Kaiser, no doctor, okay?"

Oh no. That perplexed look was back.

"I thought your name was Charlotte, and I heard the nurses calling you Dr. Charlie."

I shook my head speaking slowly. "Not here. Here I'm Charlene, okay?"

Amanda smiled brightly. "Sure, doc-er-Charlene,"— she crinkled her nose—"Do we know each other?"

"Yeah. Whatever you come up with I'll stick to it, okay? We can work out the details a little later."

"Charlene!" Amanda exclaimed, catching me off guard when she immediately enfolded me into an exuberant hug. "How crazy is it that we're running into each other here!"

I had no idea what was going on until I turned and saw Jake walking up behind me.

"You two know each other?" he asked in that velvet voice that made something inside me melt.

I was dumbstruck, because the man is even sexier the closer you get to him...or he gets to you...or whichever. I'm a sucker for a man with a goatee, and this man could call me his lollipop any day. Piercing deep brown eyes that made you feel like he was making a study of you, trying to figure you out in one glance. Sizing a person up in a matter of seconds is probably an invaluable asset as a businessman, but that look seared me. I'd estimate him at six-foot-six, putting him a few inches taller than me in these heels. I'm six feet on the nose without them. He and I would fit like a glove.

I mean Char! He and *Char* would fit like a glove.

God bless Amanda, her brain still worked. "Yeah, me and Charlene go way back. She actually used to babysit for me when I was a kid. This is crazy, right?" she laughed lightly. "Hey, I'm gonna run down and get my stuff. We'll catch up in a minute." She turned and scurried to the stairs without so much as a second glance.

"I'd better get my stuff, too," I said, trying to maintain my composure, but in my head I was imagining all kinds of things I'd like to do to this man, none of which involved being vertical...unless he liked it that way. "That was Amanda, by the way," I continued, feeling bad that she'd taken one for our newly formed team and missed a private introduction with Jake. "And I'm Charlene."

"Couldn't forget it if I wanted to," he said, taking my extended hand and pressing it to his soft lips.

The perplexed look must have jumped off Amanda's face and landed as a question on mine.

"Let's just say I'm really glad you're here," he explained as if reading my mind. "Need help with your stuff?"

I shook my head. "Wouldn't want the other girls to think I was getting any special treatment."

"No, not yet anyway."

I frowned. Between deciphering his meanings and the less-than-chaste images playing in my head, I was completely lost.

Jake smiled, a flash of perfect white teeth. "You're even prettier when you're confused."

"Well I must be the most beautiful girl here, then," I chuckled, noticing my hand was still in his.

"Without a doubt. You look great in that dress, by the way," he said, his eyes roaming over my body.

"Thank you. But I'm pretty sure you'll be telling the same thing to the other nineteen beauties in this house, Logan."

He licked his lips, and my eyes flicked to that simple but seductive gesture, then flashed back up to his.

"Maybe," he shrugged, grinning slyly. "But I wouldn't tell anyone else they'd look great without it."

I chewed my bottom lip, trying hard to suppress a smile and losing damnably. "You're gonna be a handful aren't you?"

"Up to the challenge?" he asked, cocking a brow.

"Why do you think I showed up? Could have been anywhere in the world today and I'm here with you." I pressed a kiss to his cheek and stepped back, my hand still molded to his.

"I do believe we're gonna have a great time together, angel-face."

"Looking forward to it."

With that I did my best model strut to the stairs— Char would have been proud—shoulders back, hips swaying, head high. I knew he was watching and I loved it. I went to get my—uh—*Char's* luggage. This might be a very enjoyable three days after all.

* * * *

Jake entered the master suite and shut the door behind him, the initial waves of unease he'd had at the start beginning to fade slightly. All in all he was pleased with the turnout. Most of the women he'd suggested to AJ had actually been brought on the show. The problem was he was only interested in one.

When he went to the casting he had no intention of actually finding anyone he wanted to date, and certainly not in the five minutes he'd spent in the shadows listening to Charlene Roberts talk about the legend of her eyes. But after she left it was like she'd taken all the air in the room and his attention with her. He found himself fidgeting next to AJ for the duration of the casting; watching the other women, but thinking about Charlene. Sure she was beautiful, but there was something more to her, and that's what intrigued him. He wanted to find out what it was.

Short lists of possible matches were made after every casting, and those video clips had been e-mailed to him. He'd given most of the others just a cursory glance, quickly able to spot the gold-diggers, the party girls, the fame seekers. But he found himself returning to watch Charlene's more times than he cared to admit; laughing at the wry humor of her shirt and remembering the intensity in her eyes as she told her legend with the practiced skill of a master storyteller. She was confident, engaging her hidden audience, not the camera, which was rare since most of the other girls had spoken directly to it. He'd spent many restless nights and endured a few cold showers thinking about her, forcing himself not to replay her interview; less because it was borderline obsession, and more because if he did it would only serve to drive him all the crazier. It had been the longest month of his life, anxious to start taping the show he'd dreaded doing in hopes that Charlene Roberts was just as interesting up-close-and-personal as she was at the audition—and that she was truly interested in him.

When he'd stepped out of the car and his gaze swept the crowd, hers was the only face he was searching for, and once he spotted her he was more than ready to get the show on the road. He rehashed their encounter from moments before and had to admit the tape was nothing compared to seeing her in the flesh. Even though she wore heels, he could tell she was still quite tall without them. Her eyes were a much lighter gray up close, a remarkable contrast against her smooth chocolate skin and dark hair. She smelled like something… something… sweet? Exotic? He couldn't put his finger on it, but the fragrance still playing in his nostrils sent an unexpected wave of desire through him. The dress she wore hugged her curvy shape nicely without being too revealing, and that had his blood racing, too. And when she'd pressed that kiss to his cheek her soft warm lips left the spot scorched.

The cell phone ringing in his pocket interrupted his thoughts.

"What's up," he said, already knowing who it was before he connected the call.

"So who'd you pick?"

Jake barked a laugh and paced the room, shoving his free hand into his pocket. "We've been taping for all of thirty minutes. How am I supposed to have picked from twenty girls in thirty minutes?"

"Because you're efficient. Size her up in five, talk to her for ten, by then you've decided if she's worth another fifteen or not," Marcus chuckled in reply. "I don't think I've seen you take more than half an hour before."

"Yeah, well this time I've got two months to figure it out." He rounded the corner of the bed and stood in the open sliding doorway to his balcony, seeing the women mull about the patio, drinks in hand as they familiarized themselves with their new surroundings. "I only know the names of a few so far."

"Okay, then how many are on your short list?" Marcus asked.

Apparently his best friend knew him too well. "I'm keeping all my options open, Mark." He watched as a few of the girls downed shots at the bar and cheered.

"Nah, you're lyin'. I know you, bro. I'll bet money you've already picked out the first six girls you're sending home."

Jake cringed, the downside coming back into focus. "Which is why I thought this was a bad idea in the first place."

Marcus scoffed from his end of the phone. "Bad idea my ass. Wanna trade? I've been stuck in the airport in Miami for the last four hours! Stick me in a house with twenty women and I'd die a happy man."

"I just feel a little bad that some of these girls are gonna get their feelings hurt."

"If only the tabloids knew what a big softie you are. Careful," he warned, "or you'll lose your bad boy image, J."

Jake scratched his head and grunted. "Don't remind me. You know I'm nothing like that, but since *US Weekly* has printed otherwise I'll have to play the bad boy for a while."

"My heart bleeds for you," Marcus deadpanned. "You didn't have to do this, you know. You were gonna back out when I dropped you at the casting. That you didn't makes me wonder what on earth your reason could be."

Jake thought about responding. He hadn't let Marcus watch the videos or help him choose the girls, and he certainly hadn't mentioned anything about Charlene. How could he? How could he explain being so drawn to a person whom, at the time, he'd never had a full conversation with? He opted for silence.

"Curious-er and curious-er," Marcus said thoughtfully.

"Did it ever occur to you that I just needed a break and want to have a little fun? Maybe there is no deep reason."

"Being entirely honest with oneself is a good exercise," Marcus replied simply.

"Thank you, Freud. I think I hear them calling your flight."

"Actually, you're right. Plus I know when you're avoiding a question."

"Where are you off to this time?"

Marcus groaned. "Back to Rome and then Paris, but I'll be back in LA to put in an appearance."

"Great. Then I'll put you through the wringer about *your* love life," Jake promised.

"You must be psychic, J, cause I'm workin' on that," Marcus chuckled. "Anyhow, they started boarding, so I gotta run. I'll call you when I land and see if you've come up with a reason."

It was Jake's turn to groan. "You're not gonna let this go, are you?"

"Soon as you figure it out," Marcus replied then disconnected the call.

Jake closed the phone and stuck it back in his pocket, observing all the activity going on in the backyard. It was nearly time for the mixer and almost all of the women were outside. Except for Charlene. His thoughts happily returned to his preferred topic of choice, and he found himself searching the yard for any sign of her blue dress. He tried to remind himself to give every woman a chance, when the only person he had any interest in sauntered over to the bar.

Chapter 5

The back of the house was surrounded by a multitude of plants and trees, lending a lush and exotic look to the large space, which was enclosed by a low, wood-railed, black wrought-iron gate. The ground was covered with red stone interspersed with several intricate mosaic tile patterns. This led to a large glass-tiled pool; the deep blue plates making the water look indigo in the sunlight.

As I looked about the patio I noticed Jake had yet to arrive for the mixer he'd planned. I went to the bar and prepared a Mai Tai, the only mixed drink on Char's extensive list that I remembered how to make. I don't drink much and the catchy name made me think it was the least alcoholic of all the cocktails she'd rattled off over the phone. Of course I was wrong.

There were two cabanas set up with L-shaped couches and low fire pit tables, and I went over to the one where Amanda sat sipping a drink.

"Cranberry on the rocks," she joked, holding up her glass as I took a seat in the corner of the couch next to her and watched a small group of ladies kick off their heels and sit on the edge of the pool, dangling manicured toes into the clear blue water. Another group had discovered the tequila, throwing back shots and screaming in delight.

"Keep it that way," I smiled. "At least for a couple weeks, 'kay? This soon after and you're likely to have another episode."

Amanda bobbed her head. "So why are you here, Charlene? I might have been out of it, but I seem to remember a very sexy EMT trailing after you."

"Same reason you are," I answered, ignoring her reference to Scott. "I like Jake."

As if on cue Logan stepped from the house and girls went running. Honestly, nine out of ten cardiologists would agree that these spurts of excessive exhilaration weren't good for the heart. Amanda and I kept talking when another girl joined us, sitting on the end of the couch.

"Nicole, right?" Amanda asked.

The woman smiled tersely, stirring her cocktail. Nicole was very pretty, with aquiline features and dark hair and eyes that were a perfect contrast to her caramel skin and trendy gold lame mini-dress over black tights. A gaudy ring was on her right hand, catching the sun in the cubic zirconium with every stir.

"I'm Amanda, and this is Charlene," Amanda said, trying to make small talk.

An unenthusiastic "hi" was all she got for her effort.

Amanda kept trying to speak to the woman, but it was clear to me Nicole was "that girl", the resident pain-in-the-ass who thought she was better than everyone else and tried to befriend a few girls only to turn on them later. I'd have to warn Char about her. Amanda, too.

Amanda gave up the fight and went to join the girls talking to Jake, leaving Nicole and I to our respective silences. We sat like that for a long time before she finally said, "Charlene, is it?"

I nodded.

"What do you do?" she asked, sipping the over-stirred cocktail.

"I model." I know she wasn't asking because she was interested. She wanted an in.

"Me too!" she exclaimed. "What agency?"

"Oh, I freelance. More legwork for me, but the payout is better. No agency to take a cut." I knew that much without Char's prompting.

"But do you get to work with any major designers that way?"

"A few," I responded casually, deciding to let Char give the details so she had something to talk about.

"Do they let you wear your contacts for most of the shoots? I had green ones that *Armani* wouldn't let me keep in."

"These aren't contacts."

"They're not?" She cocked her head in wonder then continued in a mocking tone. "Then you're the first black girl with *real* blue eyes I've ever met."

"They're not blue, they're gray. They just look blue because of the dress and the makeup, and they're not all that uncommon these days." I took a sip of the drink, trying to go slowly because, compared to Char, my alcohol tolerance stops at apple juice. "Maybe I'll tell you the legend sometime."

"You should tell it now. I'm sure it's a great story," Jake smiled, sliding onto the couch next to Nicole.

"Jake!" Nicole shrilled. She turned and squeezed him tightly, nearly making him spill his drink. "I'm Nicole. It's so nice to meet you, finally! I thought the wild bunch over there would never let you go."

He turned to look at the group of girls he'd just left near the pool. Two had jumped in fully clothed and were cheering as one of the others stripped to her bra and panties. They'd definitely live up to the wild bunch title.

"I managed to sneak away," he joked, turning back to us. "How about that story, Charlene?"

Nicole's pretty face dropped. "You two know each other?"

"We met earlier," a knowing smile on his lips. Damn he's sexy. I couldn't help but smile back.

He extended his arm around Nicole and she moved closer, a gesture to make sure I recognized he'd chosen to sit next to her instead of me. I pretended not to notice but knew Nicole had made her first mistake. She'd underestimated me as an opponent.

"So what were you two talking about?" Jake asked.

Nicole was off like a shot, mouth going a thousand miles a minute, talking about her modeling career and all the big names she worked for, her hopes, her dreams, all the little people she'd like to thank for this award, yadda, yadda, yadda.

Fifteen thousand miles later I thought *How much longer is he gonna let her drone on?* while trying desperately not to think of what I'd rather be doing at this exact moment in time other than listening to Nicole yammer on about how great she was.

Talk about selling yourself.

I glanced at Jake, who was responding politely, but his eyes had glazed over, making me chuckle audibly. At least he's as bored as I am. Okay, Charlie. Time to mix it up a bit.

* * * *

Jake was hanging on by a thread. Nicole obviously thought she had to tell her entire life story in the first twenty minutes. And boy could she talk! He hadn't heard a peep out of Charlene until she started chuckling and he realized she was looking at him. He tried to keep a straight face, but had to take a drink of his scotch instead.

"*Breathe*, Nicole. You haven't let anyone get a word in edgewise."

"It's not my fault if you don't speak up, Charlene," she replied defensively.

"Actually, I wasn't talking about myself. I meant Jake." He took another swallow of his scotch as she continued, "Care to tell us a little about you?"

He gave them the basics in all of three minutes. After receiving his business degree from Berkeley, he came home to run the family business, Logan Enterprises—the primary focus being a successful chain of hotels called *The Manor*. Since taking over from his father as CEO three years ago, he'd expanded LE exponentially, branching off into high-end boutique hotels at various hot spots around the world as well as a number of equally successful and skillfully located nightclubs. In addition, some savvy investments in venture capitalism and the stock market guaranteed LE would be running strong for generations to come. And he still managed to be actively involved in the three charities he'd started just after college; one to stop the spread of curable diseases in less fortunate countries; one to keep music in schools; and the last for finding a cure for paralysis.

Nicole could learn a thing or two about brevity. And humility.

"Trying to conquer the world, are we?" Charlie asked, impressed.

"That's the goal," he replied. "I see something I want and I don't stop 'til I get it."

"Do you always get what you want?"

"With frightening consistency," he asserted with a wink.

Charlie took another sip of her drink. "And what kind of things are you into when you're not conquering the world, Logan?"

Something about the way she said 'Logan', kind of sultry, rolling it off her tongue like they'd known each other for years, made Jake's body harden with desire. She was the only person to make something as formal as his last name sound like the naughtiest thing on earth, and he had the sudden urge to hear her say it over and over while he drove into her. The accompanying images were vivid, causing his pulse and breathing to quicken, and he forced his mind to focus on her question. He'd spent so much time tonight listening to people talk about themselves it was a refreshing change of pace to have a woman ask about him. It would only be polite to answer without drooling.

"Uh," he stammered, getting his breathing under control, "I'm into all—uh—kinds of music so... I go to a lot of concerts. Basketball and football games, too. I'm pretty laid back. But I'd say my favorite thing to do would be sailing. It's been a couple years, but when I get a chance to get out on my boat and it's just me and the ocean, I think that's when I'm the happiest."

Charlie could definitely relate to that. She and her mom had a pair of bikes they'd hop on whenever they could get away and ride wherever the road took them. She hadn't done that since her mom had passed, but it was one of the things in life that made her truly happy.

"I know that feeling," she said wistfully, her guard dropping. "I have a cruiser I get on whenever I need to think. Just me and the open road and after a few miles everything's crystal clear and the world's okay again." As soon as the words left her mouth she wished she could take them back because Char didn't ride a motorcycle. But the feeling that someone you'd just met really got you, really knew where you were coming from, was a comforting lure she couldn't resist.

They stared at each other a moment, an understanding passing between them.

"So, what are you looking for in a woman, Jake?" Nicole interjected boldly, turning to tuck under him further and pressing her thigh to his.

Jake reluctantly pulled his attention from Charlene to answer Nicole. "Well, I've dated a lot of models and actresses, probably because we're in a similar business so they tend to understand my fast-paced lifestyle and can keep up."

Charlie took a swallow of her Mai Tai, savoring the syrupy flavor that masked the taste of the rum as it trickled down her throat. She had to admit it was good. She licked a trace of the liquid from her lips and asked, "But what are you looking for in a woman?"

Nicole pulled a face and scoffed as though Charlie had committed the worst offense possible. "He just answered that question. Weren't you listening?"

"Intently," Charlie chirped, staring the woman in her eyes. "Had *you* been listening you'd have realized he didn't answer the question." She turned her full attention to Jake, noticing a sly grin on his face, and crossed one long leg over the other causing the already high-riding blue dress to ride a tad higher, revealing just a slip more of her inner thigh, drawing his deep brown eyes to the newly exposed bit of soft flesh. "Logan?"

He raised his gaze to her ice-gray eyes, shifting his shoulders and sipping his scotch before answering. "She's gotta be sharp... witty... smart. I mean, she doesn't have to be a rocket scientist," he said, thinking about Simone, "but an intense conversation about something other than shoes is nice."

"Well that eliminates half the girls here," Nicole giggled batting doe-eyed at him, trying to edge her way back in to the conversation.

Jake continued, looking directly at Charlie as though they were the only two people on the planet. "Confidence is good, but not arrogance. Independence. And she's gotta be one hundred percent mine."

"Submissive?" Charlie asked, cocking her head and taking another sip of her drink although a buzz was already building.

"Committed. If you're with me, you're with me."

"Does she get the same from you?"

"Without question."

Charlie bobbed her head slightly in comprehension. "And that last bit about keeping up with you, Logan. Have you ever had a woman you had to keep up with?" The question came out more as a flirtatious challenge, and she silently applauded Char's taste in alcohol for giving her the courage she'd have otherwise lacked.

That easy grin returned to Jake's face. "Not yet. But I'm looking forward to it," he replied, echoing her earlier response. He slid his arm from Nicole's shoulder and stood. "If you'll excuse me ladies, gotta make the rounds." He winked at Charlie and left the cabana to mingle with the other girls.

Nicole's plastered smile dropped the second Jake was out, shooting daggers at Charlie. "I don't know what he could possibly see in a washed up little wannabe model like you," she snarled, rolling her eyes and her neck.

Charlie threw her head back, downing the rest of her drink. "Nicole, weren't you listening? Everything he's looking for in a woman."

She left the cabana on only slightly wobbly legs, her mental faculties on full alert.

Water. She needed water "stat" to cut this buzz or she was liable to say anything. The first and last time Charlie had gotten drunk was about four years ago after the breakup with her last boyfriend; a night that started with copious amounts of plum wine, and ended with her and Char singing Mariah Carey songs on top of the bar at the Tiki Lounge, which, for the record, was not a karaoke bar. She went into the kitchen and pulled a bottle of water from the refrigerator, holding the cool plastic to her head. She'd definitely have to slow down on the Mai Tais.

Amanda came bounding past the kitchen, a bundle of excitement. "Hey Charlene! We're goin' swimming. Wanna come?"

Charlie's head was starting to spin, but staying on the show for Char meant interacting with both Jake and the other girls in the house. She took a gulp of the water and nodded. "I'll catch up with you in a minute."

* * * *

Twenty minutes later I descended the stairs feeling much better after gulping down water. I changed into an amethyst bikini with a hooded gauzy white tunic pulled over it. When I reached the deck it seemed most of the girls had settled in the Jacuzzi, trying to keep their makeup and hair perfect while clutching flutes of alcohol. But the wild bunch and Amanda were still in the pool doing flips off the diving board and hitting a beach ball back and forth.

"Hop in, Charlene," Amanda screeched, kicking her feet to stay above the water.

I dropped my towel on a deck chair and pulled the tunic over my head, placing it on the chair as well. A cameraman appeared, getting a nice shot of my ass as I bent over to secure the clasp of Char's anklet. She always had one on, but the damn thing was uncomfortable as hell.

"If that passes edits I'm gonna kill you," I threatened, taking a moment to remind myself that almost everything was being taped.

The man left quickly and I turned in time to see Jake come onto the patio wearing a pair of black boardshorts and a white t-shirt. "Food's comin' up, ladies," he announced, pulling off his shirt as he made his way to the Jacuzzi.

"That's what I'm talkin' about! Take it off, baby!" someone cheered, followed by a round of catcalls from the other ladies. I licked my bottom lip, eyes plastered to his muscular form. He was long and lean with an athletic build, cut arms and shoulders, broad sculpted pecs, perfectly ridged abs, powerful legs, and that butt! Mmmm… Definitely worthy of the 'man-cake' title. Even with the breeze I was getting hot, and I needed to jump into the pool before I dissolved into a puddle of lust or got caught drooling.

Jake chuckled, sliding effortlessly into the tub and in seconds girls were hugged up to him, embroiled in conversation.

I dove into the water, staying under a while to cool off completely. When I broke the surface a minute later Amanda was swimming close by.

"Thought you were gonna drown down there, Char," she said.

I wiped the water from my eyes and leaned back to let it organize my hair. It would be a curly mess in a little while, but I didn't care. One of the girls from the wild bunch, Larisa, swam over to us.

"O. M. G. You guys will never guess what's happening," she said dramatically as we all swam to the edge of the pool. "I just overheard that girl Danielle on the phone with some guy named Terrance, and they so don't sound like friends."

Amanda beat me to the punch. "What did she say?"

"First she said something like 'are you sure this is gonna help my career?' and then I heard her say 'you know I don't even like him, Terrance,' and then after a while she told him 'I love you, baby'."

"You gotta tell Jake," Amanda said and turned to me, "Don't you think?"

Had I not been in a similar situation as Danielle I'd have nodded my little head off, but as it stood I was a bit dumbstruck. Of course I should tell him, but what would happen if someone found out about my own deception? Hell, Amanda knows I'm doctor Charlie, not model Charlene. Maybe she thought I was here because I really like Jake. I reasoned I was only gonna be here three days. Char would be here soon and the whole deception thing wouldn't even be an issue.

"Of course you have to tell him," I agreed after a very pregnant pause. "And you better do it soon. If this is anything like last season there's gonna be an elimination tonight."

"You think so?" Amanda asked, getting nervous. "So soon?"

I nodded. "So get a move on, Larisa."

She pulled her short frame up the edge of the pool and out, and padded over to the hot tub, her wet footsteps slapping the ground as she went. After a few minutes Jake climbed out, dried off, and followed Larisa inside.

"Food's ready," a member of the catering crew called out ten minutes later, and the ladies filed into the house.

"You comin', Char?" Amanda asked, drying off quickly and slinging the towel about her waist.

"In a minute."

She went into the house to get a plate and I dove under the water again. It's nice having a pool this large to yourself, swimming about unimpeded. I leisurely swam a few laps then climbed up the stairs. When I reached the deck chair Jake was coming back out of the house, an irritated look on his face.

I grabbed my belongings and walked over to him.

"You okay?"

He spun to face me, surprise overshadowing irritation.

"My bad. Didn't mean to startle you," I said, holding up my hands in apology.

"I thought everyone had gone inside to eat."

"And so you came out here to fume? Not that I know you that well, but you look bothered."

Jake nodded slightly, crossing his arms over his chest and leaning back on his heels. "Just got some bad news about our girl Danielle. It seems she has a boyfriend and is only on the show to further her acting career."

I instantly felt horrible for him, not because of Danielle but because of me and Char. I couldn't imagine what it would be like to have people constantly using you, and to know I was one of them... "You talked to her about it?"

"Of course. I wanted to give her a fair chance to defend herself, and she flat out lied to me. I've got multiple businesses around the world. I deal with different personalities almost daily, and everyone is trying to get something for nothing. I know when someone's lyin' to me."

He admitted to being bothered, but I noticed his tone was too calm. "You're not mad though, huh?"

"What makes you think that?" he frowned.

"I said you looked bothered, not angry. Plus your voice is calm. And you've got too many women here to lose sleep over one."

A grin curved his lips and he laughed softly. "You can read me like a book, Charlene. Better keep my eye on you. You're right. I don't know her well enough to be angry. She's just gotta go." He looked down at me, his mood changing in a heartbeat. "Did you eat already?"

"Nope. You hungry?"

"I could eat. That bikini is *very* sexy, by the way," he said, draping his arm about my shoulder and squeezing me to him, making my heart race as he led me into the house. God, the things this man does to me and I've only just met him today!

"Thank you, but if you keep paying me compliments you'll have a hard time getting rid of me, Logan." I slid my arm around his waist, the feel of his toned obliques beneath my fingers sending little jots of electricity through me.

"That's kind of the idea, angel-face." He brushed his lips lightly across my temple like he'd done it all his life. "That's kind of the idea."

Now what am I supposed to say to that?

Chapter 6
{Day 2 on Free Money}

I woke up early the morning after the first elimination ceremony, which was nothing like the ceremonies last season. Apparently Jake does things his own way around here. Last year all the girls lined up in two rows, the top row standing on a platform like they were taking a class picture. Then the guy called each girl down to get a glass of champagne and asked if she wanted to continue on the journey with him. If you didn't get a glass, you were off the show. That's basically how all the reality shows do it, the only variation being the champagne, or a chain, or a picture, or whatever.

Not Logan. Last night we all lined up in the rows, but instead of calling us down one by one, Jake said a few words, called down two girls, Susana and Tasha, said he didn't feel anything romantic for either one of them and sent them on their merry little way. The rest of us were stunned that he didn't cut Danielle, until moments later he called her down and said she had to go for deceiving him. Then he asked the rest of us, "Anyone else here for exposure?" When no one moved he said, "Anyone else got a boyfriend? Cause the door's right there. Don't waste my time."

We all stood there in that tense moment, eyes shifting slightly to see if anyone would be foolish enough to move, then he finally said, "All right then, ladies, come get your glasses."

And then there were seventeen.

There was a toast and cheer for the cameras, a crewmember yelled "Cut" and the first episode was ready for edits. Then we all went back inside, film was changed, equipment checked, and filming for episode two began. It's kind of a weird process, but eventually you forget the cameras are even there.

While my roomies snored the morning away I pulled myself out of bed, brushed my teeth and washed my face, threw on some workout clothes and headed for the gym on the second floor. It was deserted as expected, so I had my choice of equipment. The wall clock read 6:13. A half an hour on the treadmill and another half on the bike would do me good. Maybe some light weights. I usually hit the gym at odd hours around my shifts at Kaiser, so as bizarre as it sounds a continuous workout is a real treat!

I opened the windows letting in cold morning air, and pushed the door closed. After stretching lightly I selected my workout playlist on my iPod, hit shuffle and connected it to the dock. Then I hopped on the treadmill as The Coasters' *Down in Mexico* came through the recessed wall speakers.

After thirty minutes I had run almost six miles and was ready for the bike. I got off the treadmill, shirt soaked and feeling great. I had gone nearly three miles in eight minutes on the bike when Imelda May started singing her rockabilly song *Big Bad Handsome Man.* I love this song, and belted it out at the top of my lungs as I shifted gears, my thighs burning while I peddled the bike up to speed.

...Leaves me wanting mo-ore and mo-ore!
Cause he's my big, bad, handsome maaan, yeah...

I sang, eyes closed, peddling hard, so engrossed in the song I didn't immediately realize the music had stopped. I opened my eyes and saw Jake standing near the iPod clapping.

"Mornin', angel-face! Singing a song about me? I'm touched."

"Oh, god! How long have you been in here?" Talk about mortifying.

"Just long enough for your last performance," he laughed.

"So now you know why I model and not sing." I'd have to tell Char, who had a beautiful voice that I'd blown it for her. "You usually up this early?"

He leaned his tall frame against the wall, watching me as I worked up a good froth. "Yeah, although apparently I need to be up a little earlier to catch your morning show."

"Sorry, chief, there won't be any repeat performances," I grimaced, continuing to peddle. "Were you eating breakfast?"

He shook his head. "Just got back from a run. I haven't had breakfast yet. Wanna join me?"

"Does that mean you want me to make you breakfast?" I teased. "Because I cook worse than I sing."

"Really?"

"No, I'm a great cook. And of course I'll join you." I stopped the bike and dismounted, wiping my face and hair on the towel and grabbing my iPod from the dock. "How'd you know I was in here?"

"You kiddin'? Heard you callin' the cows on my way up to take a shower," he laughed, holding the door open for me as I walked past him. "You can join me for that, too, if you want."

"Oh, no. You gotta at *least* feed me first," I half-joked, almost tempted to take him up on the offer. Not that I'd have such an intimate relationship with a total stranger after knowing him less than twenty-four hours, but the naughty side of my brain had been playing out fantasies of Jake since our first encounter yesterday. The physical attraction was obvious, the sexual attraction blatant, but I wouldn't put myself in that position. Or Char for that matter. In fact, I should be kicking myself for flirting this heavily with him. Char would have some big shoes to fill.

"Fine," Jake dragged like a kid being asked to do a chore he didn't want to. "First breakfast, *then* a shower."

I noticed he sounded like he was only half-joking, too.

We went downstairs to the huge gourmet kitchen. We both went to the sink and washed our hands; I washed mine up to my elbows out of habit and got a raised brow from Jake. As I was walking to the refrigerator a strong arm encircled my waist, pulling me off course.

"Go sit down," Jake ordered, stepping around me and opening the door.

"I was joking, Logan! For real, I can cook."

He peered over the door of the fridge and raised a skeptical brow.

"Really. I'm a good cook," I protested weakly with a giggle—I was doing that a lot lately—taking a seat at the island. "Ask my sister!"

Oh hell. Hadn't meant to mention her. Char and I didn't have a contingency plan for the topic of siblings. I had no idea whether she wanted him to know she had a twin or not.

Jake pulled eggs, peppers, cheese, ham, and milk from the fridge, kicking the door shut with his foot.

"You like omelets?" He asked walking about the kitchen, gathering utensils and spices.

"Uh huh." I watched him crack eggs into the bowl and chop up the peppers with obvious ease. Sexy *and* can cook. God, you're killing me!

"I'm sure you boil a mean pot of water, and you'll have lots of time to show me later. But I wanted to do something for you. Sort of an apology since I didn't get a chance to learn much about you yesterday at the mixer."

"Thanks, Logan. That's really sweet," I said, genuinely meaning it. "But at least you learned *everything* about Nicole."

He rolled his eyes and chuckled. "Don't remind me. That girl would talk about herself all day if I let her." He set a pan on the stove and went back to the fridge. "So you have a sister?"

Crap. "Yeah, just the one."

"Older? Younger?"

"Younger."

Not a lie, technically. Then again, what's eight minutes?

"You two look alike?"

"You could say that."

"What does she do?" He poured a little orange juice into two flutes and topped them both with champagne.

"Annoy the hell out of me. It's the job of all little sisters, isn't it?" I laughed, trying to divert the conversation, realizing too late that I was supposed to be answering as Charlene, the younger sister. I'd have to pay more attention.

He poured the eggs into the pan and sprinkled the ingredients over them. Then he handed me a glass.

"To sunrise singing," he joked, clicking his glass against mine.

"Ha. Ha."

He chuckled before continuing the conversation with a smile. "I'm an only child."

"Ahh, so that explains it."

"What?" he asked, frowning as he flipped the omelets.

"Conquering the world. Only children tend to go one of two ways. Either they're really spoiled and pampered, or they're really strong leaders with a hidden sensitive side. Lucky for you I like leaders."

"Then I guess it works out for both of us, huh, angel-face," he stated, sliding an omelet onto each plate and setting one in front of me. He grabbed two forks from a drawer and handed me one, then brought his plate to sit beside me.

"Mmmm. This is so good, Logan," I said, savoring the first bite.

"I really like the way you say my name."

"Jake?" I squeaked around the bite of food.

He shook his head then turned his body toward me completely, resting one foot on the bottom rung of my stool. "Logan. It rolls off your tongue like honey, like you *enjoy* saying it. Do you?"

I stared into his eyes, watching as his pupils started dilating. Medically speaking this could mean any number of things. Maybe he was having a response to some sort of external stressor, or that the room was darkening, although neither of us had turned off the lights. Or, it could mean he was aroused. Bingo. I dropped my eyes to the pulse point in his throat, noting the erratic throbbing, and dragged my peepers up in time to catch him licking his lips. The notion that I was turning this man on was turning me on, and adrenaline shot through my body in time with the alarms going off in my head. I needed to pull away fast. But try as I might, I couldn't. Or wouldn't.

"You always this forward, Logan?" I purred, unable to resist.

His lids lowered to half-mast, and he licked his lips again as if hearing me say his name was giving him the best ear-gasm ever.

"I won't forget that you didn't answer the question, and I told you before, when I know what I want I go after it—"

"And you get it with frightening consistency," I finished. "So what exactly is it you want?"

"You."

"How?" My mouth moves faster than my brain sometimes. The way it was intended was not the way it was interpreted.

"Any way you'll let me," he retorted silkily, that easy grin returning to his face.

I playfully slapped his thigh, cutting my eyes at him. "That's not the way I meant that and you know it. I mean in what capacity? Just friends? Friends with benefits? Or something more? Cause I'm here for something more."

He didn't respond, so I continued in a rush.

"We did just meet, and I can't imagine you've developed any serious feelings for me in less than a day. So, how and why, Jake?" I really hated doing that. Making a man think when all the blood was flowing *away* from his brain wasn't exactly fair. But I had the feeling any second now we'd be on this countertop doing all the things I wanted him to do to me, and then Char would be screwed. Well *I'd* be screwed, but you know what I mean.

Our eyes locked, deep brown to ice gray, each watching as lust built in the other, when Nicole rounded the corner and entered the kitchen. We both promptly returned to our omelets like teenagers caught making out under the bleachers.

"Good morning, Jake," she chirped as she came around the island, ignoring me completely. "How'd you sleep, baby?"

I chuckled under my breath and Jake poked me in the side, chewing furiously to keep from laughing.

"Omelets?" she asked, looking at our plates. "You cook, Charlene?"

"Actually, Jake made these, and the mimosas." I can't lie. I got some satisfaction out of that. "They're *really* good, too." I never skimp on the frosting.

Nicole poked her lip out into a pout. "Can I have some of yours, baby?" she whined, hugging him from behind and dropping her head on his shoulder. Then she cringed and backed away quickly, her voice returning to normal. "Why are you damp and sticky?"

"Not for the reasons I was hoping," he mumbled.

I nearly choked on my omelet.

"I didn't get to shower after my run. Which reminds me about my earlier offer, Charlene," he said the lust still simmering in his eyes.

"Answers first, Jake." Finishing my food and downing the drink, I pushed myself off the barstool and carried my dishes to the sink.

Nicole started jabbering away as I cleaned up. Things were starting to get complicated. When Char came in a few days she'd be embroiled in a full-blown physical relationship if I weren't careful. I pushed away a feeling of melancholy and refocused my attention on the reason I was here.

This is Charlene's thing, Charlie. You're just a stand-in for the next couple days. Anything you feel for Jake is a fabrication for Char's sake. Okay? Okay? Okay.

Nicole came over and dumped Jake's dishes in the sink causing the soapy water to splash up my arms, and then went back to chatting him up. The girl was purposefully grating on my nerves, but I refuse to let her see me bothered. I'd get my own back. I finished the dishes, drained the water and dried my hands.

Leaving the sink I went behind Jake, dropping a quick kiss on his neck and interrupting his boredom, said a quick, "Thanks for breakfast," and headed out of the kitchen.

"You never answered my question, Charlene," he called after me, stopping me in my tracks. "Do you enjoy it?"

He asked that loaded question in a neutral tone that belied its origin. I glanced at Nicole who looked upset that I'd taken his attention and that she was once again out of the loop. Pleased, I turned back to Jake, seeing that same intensity in his eyes. "Yeah, Logan. I enjoy it."

I wasn't lying.

* * * *

A few hours later we had our first challenge, a trivia contest about all things Logan. Since there were seventeen ladies left, we divided into two groups of six and a group of five. Each group chose a leader and was given a thick binder with random facts about Jake. The questions ranged from the obvious "what does he do for a living" to the less-familiar "pet's name as a kid." We had an hour to learn the binder before the challenge started.

I was in the group of five, which wasn't a problem because I have a knack for cramming info into my head in a short time—it's how I survived med-school. But I'm supposed to be Char who is less detail-oriented, so I decided to try not to answer all the questions. And I thought it best if I keep away from Logan for the rest of my short stay here.

My team, the pink team, consisted of Amanda, Lori, Tameka, and our team leader Nicole. As luck would have it she drew the short straw. I had to grin and bear it through an hour of Nicole's "coaching". Now I'm really hoping we win this challenge quickly so I can go on this date and get away from this girl. She's annoying personified.

We took a ride from the mansion to a TV studio in Burbank and were met with a full audience and host who went over the rules of the game. Each team was stationed behind the booth of their color—pink, blue, or yellow. The rules were that the host would spin a wheel with different categories and when it was your team's turn you'd have to answer a question from that category in ten seconds. Like Math-letes with hot chicks.

After thirty questions, our team and the yellow team were tied at sixty-five points. The blue team had almost all the party girls on it, so I kind of saw it coming. They spent more time getting dressed for the challenge than reading the binder. I offered enough answers to keep us in the game, but other than that I let the other girls have at it.

"Time for the speed round," the host said excitedly. "So each of our two remaining teams need to choose one girl to come up to the buzzer for a face-off. Whoever gets the most questions right will win it for their team. I'll give you a few moments to decide."

We huddled up.

"I think Charlene should do it," Amanda said without hesitation.

Nicole grimaced, her ever-present attitude showing its face for the umpteenth time. "But she hasn't answered anything all day."

"Are you kidding? She's the reason we're still in the contest. She answered all the hard ones!"

Did I mention I like Amanda? The girl's got spunk.

"I think Charlene should do it, too," Lori agreed. "She seems to be calm under pressure."

"Do you *want* to do it, Nicole?" I asked, cutting to the chase.

She didn't answer.

"Look at it this way. If we win you'll still get the extra time with Jake for being the leader. If we lose, you can blame it all on me. It's a win-win situation for you."

Nicole thought it over, and just as the host called for the contestants she blurted, "I think you should do it," as if she had come up with the idea in the first place. "But you better win. I want that time."

It seriously crossed my mind to lose on purpose, but then I'm not really the spiteful type. "As you command, your highness." I bowed mockingly and left the booth, hearing Amanda snickering behind me.

I was going up against a girl named Cynthia, one of the quieter girls in the house who, if I remember correctly, was in grad school studying philosophy. This would be fun.

"Okay ladies. I'll ask a question and whoever buzzes in first and gives the correct answer gets a point for her team," the host explained. "If you get it wrong the other team gets a chance to answer. The speed round is sixty seconds. Wait for me to call out your team color before answering, okay?"

We nodded and shook hands.

"Sixty seconds on the clock. Time starts after I read the first question. Ready? What is Jake's middle name?"

I slapped the buzzer.

"Pink," the host said.

"Anthony."

"Yes. What was his first pet?"

I slapped it again.

"Yellow."

Crap.

"A bull dog?" Cynthia answered unsure.

"No. Pink?"

"A pit bull named Sammy."

"Yes. His favorite pastime?"

"Pink."

"Sailing." I knew that from yesterday.

"Yes. The location of his newest club? Pink."

"Japan."

"Yes. The name of that club? Pink again."

"Koodori Doragon or the Dancing Dragon."

"Yes! His brother's name? Yellow."

"Andrew."

Did Cynthia even *see* the book?

"No. Pink?"

"He doesn't have a brother."

"Yes. What school did he graduate from? Yellow."

"UCLA."

"No. Pink?'

"UC Berkeley."

"Right again!" The host exclaimed just after the buzzer sounded. "And that's the end of it. After that *dominating* speed round, the winner is the pink team!"

The audience cheered and my team gathered around and hugged me. Even Nicole, although I'm sure I'll be her favorite person on earth until just after her extra time with Jake.

Logan appeared next to the host, looking fine as ever in a pair of black jeans, sneakers and a polo shirt. "Great job, pink team. Since you ladies won the first challenge, I'm taking the five of you on the first date tomorrow. And Nicole, as team leader, I've got something special planned for you."

Nicole beamed.

"So I'll see everyone back at the house later then, okay?" He turned and left the studio and we piled into the vans, the ladies on my team chatting excitedly about what they were wearing for the date with Logan and guessing where we'd go and what we'd do.

As we drove back to the mansion I stared out the window; the relief that this charade was about to be over tempered only by the melancholy that this charade was about to be over. I promised three days and they were up. I got a couple free nights in a mansion, swam in a huge pool, met some nice people, and in a few hours I'd be back at home working on mom's bike, enjoying my real vacation.

Three days, three days, three days, I reminded myself.

But three days suddenly weren't enough.

Chapter 7
{*Day 3*}

It might be Los Angeles, but mornings are still pretty cold. Jake and I didn't cross paths this morning, which was fine by me. It would make it easier when Char came in today. I had a nice workout—sans singing—took a hot shower, and pulled on jeans and a sweatshirt. I pulled my curls back into their customary ponytail and slid on my black slippers.

It had to be near eight and I was starving, so I went down to the kitchen to scrounge up some food. A couple girls had already made breakfast and were sitting around the pool, the steam from their coffee mugs mixing with the smoke from their cigarettes.

I went into the pantry to grab the box of hot chocolate when Amanda snuck up behind me, poking me in my sides, making me jump and shriek.

"Morning, Char!" she chirped.

Sometime last night I had gotten over my despondency at leaving and I was feeling pretty happy. I gave her a quick hug. "Hey Amanda. How ya feelin' this morning?"

"I feel just great! Jake's takin' us on a date! Me and my best mate! You know I can't wait! Hope we stay out real late!" She did this rhyming with a little singsong in her voice and an equally goofy dance, giggling the whole time. Amanda's got one of those infectious laughs. Once she gets started she keeps going, and before you know it you're giggling, too.

So there we were, still giggling at her song as I filled the kettle with water and put it on the stove to boil.

"Hot chocolate?" I asked, pulling a mug from the cupboard.

"After all this time you still remember it's my favorite thing to wake up to in the morning," she said, laughing at our charade.

I rolled my eyes and chuckled. "Some things a good babysitter never forgets." I grabbed a second mug and brought them both to the stove, shaking the packets of cocoa so the powder wouldn't fly all over when I ripped them open.

She went into the pantry again, emerging with a bag. "You forgot the best part. Marshmallows." She came over and upturned the bag over her mug, letting a rush of confections fall in.

I shook my head and grinned. "That's straight sugar on top of sugar. You might as well swallow a box of sugar cubes whole!"

Amanda grabbed a handful of the tiny sweets from the bag and tossed a couple into the air, catching both expertly in her mouth with a wide smile. "Come on, Char, live a little. Hot chocolate isn't exactly tomato juice to begin with."

A marshmallow flew my way and I caught it between my front teeth.

"Two points!" Amanda screeched enthusiastically. "One for the catch, the other for style. Front teeth. That's hard stuff. 'Kay, my turn."

I pulled a few from the bag and tossed one across the room at her. She did a lovely pirouette and grabbed the confection from the air, then took a graceful bow. "Ta da!"

"Ooh! Four points!" I said excitedly, clapping. "Nice spin! Like a real ballerina."

"Years of ballet," she said lightly then continued in mock disbelief, one hand on her hip, "and my parents think a degree in dance is such a waste!"

I couldn't help but laugh. She reminded me so much of Char, carefree and creative. I'd definitely miss Amanda when I left. Two marshmallows went in opposite directions only seconds apart. I hopped from one foot to the other, nabbing both and bumping into an irritated Nicole coming in from the patio.

"Sorry," I giggled, chewing the spongy treats. "Didn't see you."

The look on her face indicated my apology had not been accepted. I couldn't care less.

"If you two kids wanna play around, don't you think you could do it outside the kitchen? You'd think someone as old as you would have grown up already, Charlene."

Amanda tossed another marshmallow in her mouth. "You're a real tight-ass, aren't you? She apologized, didn't she? And just how old are you, Nicole? Twenty-six goin' on ninety?"

Did I mention I like Amanda?

"Toss me another one, Char," she said, not letting Nicole stop our fun.

I turned away from her and threw it high over my shoulder, spinning just in time to see Jake nudge Amanda out the way and catch it in his mouth.

"A marshmallow contest and no one called me?" he pouted, making the most adorable little face. Amanda giggled as he draped his arm around her shoulder. "I should have known you two were behind this," he grinned.

I threw another at Amanda then tossed one in the air for myself.

"Good morning, baby," Nicole crooned, rushing over to hug him in spite of the fact that Amanda was still tucked under his wing.

"We would have called you, Jake, but grandma Nikki here was giving us youngsters a proper scolding for playing in the kitchen," Amanda chimed in, then continued to Nicole, "ain't that right, Methuselah?"

Nicole glared at the younger girl from under Jake's other arm.

"Well, that's gotta be at least two points to Logan for the steal, " I said removing the kettle from the stove and filling both mugs with the boiling water. "Although not much for style. You gotta spice it up a bit if you wanna compete with us pros, Jake."

He threw me a glance I couldn't read then smiled down at Amanda. "You guys ready to go out today?"

Amanda nodded, bouncing on her toes. "Where are we going?"

"Gonna grab some lunch up the coast. Nothing major," he said casually.

I could see Nicole's excitement deflate and decided to call her out on it. "Disappointed, Nicole? You thought Jake was gonna charter a flight to London or something?"

He glanced down at her as she pressed her lean frame into his chest, standing on her tippy-toes and looking up at him seductively. "I'm just ready to get that extra-special somethin' you promised me."

Amanda rolled her eyes and sighed theatrically, making me chuckle as I stirred both cups of cocoa.

"Right," Jake said blandly. "Should be fun. Hey, could you excuse us for a minute? I need to talk to Charlene."

Amanda waggled her brows at me then retrieved her mug from the counter. "Sure, Jake. See you later."

Nicole groaned. "Fine, but don't take forever," she ordered, glaring at me then stomping out of the kitchen.

I took a sip of the cocoa, savoring the rich chocolate taste and peering at Jake over the rim of the mug. When he was sure we were alone he took a seat at the island then motioned for me to join him.

I settled onto the barstool placing the mug on the countertop, our relative positions reminiscent of yesterday, right down to his foot resting on the bottom rung of my chair. He was so close I could feel the heat from his body, or maybe that was my own body on fire. Either way, it was getting hot. "What's up?"

"I was thinking about you last night," he began, making my heart leap into my throat. "And I owe you an apology."

Confusion washed over me. "What for?"

"Yesterday. You might have gotten the impression that I'm just tryin' to get in your pants, and—"

"And·now you're *not* tryin' to get in my pants?" I interrupted, feigning concern.

He shook his head grinning. "You know what I mean."

"No I don't, Logan," I said giving him a vacuous doe-eyed stare, my voice light. "I haven't got a clue what you mean, aside from the bit about you tryin' to get in my pants, of course. That I understood completely, I think."

"You're enjoying this, aren't you?" he asked, his brown eyes twinkling.

"Immensely," I winked. "Gotta keep you on your toes. But just so you're not tossing and turning all night, worried that I misunderstood your gallant intentions, I didn't think that was your endgame."

"Good, because I really want to get to know you, and I want you to know that from here on out I'll be the perfect gentleman," he said, raising three fingers of one hand and saluting. "Scout's honor."

I stared back unconvinced.

"Well, maybe 'perfect gentleman' is stretching it a bit," he chuckled.

"That's my Logan," I replied cheerily, reaching out to pat his cheek. He turned his head slightly to kiss my palm, a shiver rushing through me, and I reluctantly dropped my hand back to my lap.

We sat there a while staring at each other, the attraction between us building in the complete silence. I could hear my heart pounding in my head and my breathing quickened, until the intensity of his gaze made me turn away. Needing an interruption, I reached for the mug when he caught my hand, tangling my fingers in his and bringing my eyes back to him. When he spoke, his voice was low.

"Just a little longer, angel-face. I'm enjoying the view."

I looked up at him, a corner of my lower lip secured between my teeth, forcing myself not to lean forward and kiss him. His lips looked soft and inviting, the lower one just begging me to draw it in my mouth and suck it mercilessly. By the look on his face, he was fighting a similar battle.

"Why do you call me that?" My voice sounded distant in my ears. He was lazily rubbing his thumb against my trapped fingers, sending little spirals of heat through me.

"Your eyes. They kinda glow like halos," he replied in a low smooth voice. "They're really lovely. It's hard not to get lost in 'em."

I swallowed hard, forcing my tongue to work. "I'm no angel, Logan." I was starting to feel bad about my deception, but I also had a sudden need to break the spell his sexy eyes were casting.

A devilish grin turned his lips. "I certainly hope not." He leaned toward me; the promise of his kiss finally nearing its end, when Nicole came back into the kitchen, causing him to divert the landing from my lips to my cheek. "Another time," he whispered, his warm breath against the shell of my ear, the soft feel of his lips on my face and the scent of his cologne sending new ripples of anticipation even lower in my already responding body. He released my fingers, leaving my hand feeling cold and aching to reach out for him again.

Nicole dramatically cleared her throat, and I could have sworn I heard Jake groan.

"Are you two done, yet, Jake?" she asked annoyed.

He peered over his shoulder at her then slid off the stool. "For now. I'm gonna go get ready for this afternoon. See you both later." He left the room and Nicole, who glowered at me from a distance.

"Of all the girls in this house, I hope he doesn't choose you," she hissed then turned on her heel to find some of the other girls to gossip with.

I grabbed my cup of cocoa, taking a sip of the chilling liquid in an attempt to cool my warm body. I was playing with fire the longer I stayed in this house. But how in the hell were Char and I supposed to switch at a lunch at some undisclosed location up the coast? I shrugged, a small smile playing on my lips. I'd just have to call Char and tell her it would take a little longer.

Darn.

* * * *

Lunch up the coast. Nothing major. Yeah right.

I don't think Logan knows how to do anything low-key.

The six of us—Nicole, Amanda, Lori, Tameka, Jake, and I—were picked up from the mansion by a sleek black limo, where we sipped champagne and ate strawberries on our way to what I thought would be our final destination. Except, we headed away from the ocean and drove into downtown LA.

Logan helped each of us from the limo and led us into the Westin Bonaventure, one of the premier hotels in the area. Stepping inside is like being in a city inside the city, with its upscale shops and restaurants, modern interior, multiple towers; lunch here would be nothing to scoff at. We followed Logan through the atrium—Nicole and Lori clinging to his arms—where the concierge greeted him, an older man with a cherubic face named Daniel. Daniel ushered us to a private elevator, and as the doors closed Amanda asked, "Where are we going?"

"To lunch," Jake said simply, inserting a small key into a slot and turning it.

The carriage rose and Amanda pressed on. "But you said lunch up the coast."

Jake's lips quirked into a smile.

The rest of the six hundred foot ascent was made in silent expectation, and when the doors slid open we were met with sunlight and a strong breeze—on the roof of the Westin. Twenty feet away sat a large white helicopter, *Logan Ent.* written in emerald green script on the tail boom.

"Hey, Jake," a small woman waved as our group approached. She had caramel skin, short dark hair, and deep-set brown eyes that crinkled a bit when she smiled.

He gave her an affectionate hug then turned to introduce us. "Ladies, this is my good friend Izzie, who is also my personal pilot. Izzie, I'd like you to meet Nicole, Amanda, Lori, Tameka, and Charlene."

She took the time to shake each of our hands and give us a warm smile before adding, "I hope you ladies are being good to him. He's a really great guy."

"You bribed your pilot, Logan?" I joked, shaking my head as I released Izzie's hand.

He threw his head back and barked a laugh, a sound I'd really come to enjoy. "Charlene and Amanda don't cut me any slack, Iz. These first couple days have been a mess."

"You wouldn't know what to do without us, Jake," Amanda grinned.

Izzie looked at the three of us and decided to join in the fun. "Well, now that you mention it, he did welsh on a bet once."

"Izzie," Jake warned.

"What was the bet?" I asked.

Izzie smiled, crossing her arms over her chest and leaning back on her heels. "Bet me I couldn't fly upside down."

"You fly upside down?"

She shook her head morosely. "I *flew* upside down. Once. I've been banned from doing it again."

"You nearly killed us!" Jake exclaimed, eyes twinkling with amusement.

"Like I knew the motor would stall," she shrugged nonchalantly. "It shouldn't have stalled, but things happen."

"So no flying upside down today?" I verified.

Izzie looked hopefully at Jake who shook his head voraciously. Izzie sighed.

"No, Char. No flying upside down ever again," Jake said, helping us into the cabin of the plush craft.

He sat between Amanda and I, letting us have the window seats so we could see the view en route to our "nothing major" lunch up the coast.

The other ladies were putting on the headsets needed for in-flight communication when I leaned over and asked, "Isn't this a private launch?"

Jake whispered back. "I might own a share or two of this property."

"Wow! You really are trying to take over the world, huh?" I smiled, nudging him in the side playfully then reached for my headset.

"How'd you know this was a private launch?"

Crap. I'd really have to stop talking or I'd be in a world of trouble. When you're trying to pull a switcheroo, it's best to say as little as possible so you don't get caught in a lie. I couldn't tell him I knew it was private because this heliport was listed in our emergency room as a possible launch for medicopters.

"I had a shoot here once," I lied. I was getting really sick of lying, especially to Jake. "Where are we going?"

He settled more comfortably in the soft leather seat, securing his seat belt as the chopper began its nearly vertical ascent. Then he glanced at his watch. "You'll know in about forty minutes."

* * * *

A short helicopter ride up the coast from Los Angeles is the beautiful seaside city of Carmel. Known for its dramatic coastline, stunning white sand beaches, and a gypsy charm, the serene little town tucked just south of Monterey was the destination for Jake's first date. Once the chopper touched down in an empty grass field, a white and gold van arrived to transport the party the short distance to the Rocky Point Restaurant.

Nestled on the lush green hillside, the group was seated on the restaurant's ocean terrace, watching the waves curl and crash against the shore below as they waited for their meals to arrive.

"This is amazing, Jake," Amanda gasped, taking it all in. "Do you come here often?"

"I haven't been here in a while. But it's just as beautiful as I remember it," he smiled. "Glad you like it."

Nicole moved her chair a hair closer to Jake's and Charlie suppressed a giggle as he suppressed a groan. "Thank you, baby. This was so sweet," she purred.

"You're welcome," he managed, flashing his eyes across the table to Charlie. "So, tell me more about yourselves. Lori, you said you work for an accounting firm in Illinois, right?"

Charlie tuned out of the conversation, taking slow sips of her wine as she enjoyed the view. Through the hazy sky, the Big Sur Lighthouse was barely visible to the south and as she looked down the cliff-face into the ocean, a pod of brown pelicans dove into the water in search of their own midday meals. She stared at the fuss, all the birds splashing as their bodies disappeared beneath the blue-green water then bobbing like feathered corks as they broke the surface with their leathery beaks stretched by fish and saltwater.

Her thoughts drifted to a fifth-grade field trip. The class had gone whale watching, their boat leaving from Newport Beach early that morning packed with kids bundled like they were going to the snow instead of a few miles out to sea. Charlene was dragging their mother to the concession stand to get a bag of candy for Charlie—her love for candy being how she'd earned the nickname 'sweets' from her twin—and their father was holding Charlie as she leaned over the rail, watching the churning water with great concern that they'd drive over the animals. She remembered chasing Char around the boat, and seeing her parents cuddled together at the railing as they looked out at the sea. They'd seen so many whales that day, and a couple dolphins, and lots of birds—pelicans included—and it would always be the fondest memory of her childhood. It was one of the last times they would all be together.

Charlie smiled wistfully at the memory, her eyes searching the azure expanse for any signs of whales or dolphins or happy families on site-seeing boats in the distance.

"Char." Amanda shook her arm, jarring her from her musings.

She forced herself back to the moment noticing the five other faces at the table had their attention on her and the meals had been served. "I'm sorry, I was… watching the pelicans diving," she admitted sheepishly. "What were you saying?"

Jake smiled. "I was wondering how close everyone is with their family. Lori mentioned she wasn't sure how her parents would take her bringing me home because of our age difference. Nicole insists her parents would love to have me in the family," he said with only mild sarcasm then chuckled, "Amanda said she didn't care. Tameka thinks her parents wouldn't mind. So you're the only one left."

Charlie shifted uncomfortably in her seat. "Umm… my sister will love you," she stated, knowing it to be an absolute truth since it was Char who wanted to meet Jake in the first place. "My parents… they would have been happy with whoever made me happy… even you, Logan," she teased, taking a sip of wine to recover from a moment of despondency.

Jake met her gray eyes, catching the hitch in her voice with her last statement. He questioned her with a frown, cocking his head slightly.

"My father was killed in a car accident when I was about ten," Charlie said quietly, absently flaking the seared salmon with her fork. "But I think he would have liked you. My mom… my mom—uh—mom… died… about nine months ago. Cancer." She put a forkful of food in her mouth and chewed, although she really didn't taste it.

"I'm so sorry to hear that," Jake said genuinely as Amanda squeezed Charlie's arm in support.

"It happens. I know they're still watching over me." She forced some levity into her voice. "So lucky for you, Logan, you've only got my sister to contend with. And believe me, where you're concerned, she'll be a push-over."

"Glad to hear it," he joked in return, understanding her need to move past the matter. The other ladies began talking politely amongst themselves, and Charlie continued eating her food, turning her head to stare at the pelicans again, hoping to recapture her memories.

Jake couldn't pull his eyes off her. His heart ached for her, thinking about his own parents and how much they meant to him. Sure they drove him crazy, always meddled in his personal life, but to lose them... he wasn't sure he could handle it, let alone with the strength and grace Charlene had. It made him admire her even more.

"So, where's that special surprise I get, Jake," Nicole cooed, breaking into his thoughts a moment later.

He smiled politely and grabbed his scotch. "Just this way," he answered, taking her hand as he rose from the table. "Excuse us, ladies." He ushered Nicole to a footpath that curved down the hillside, the end not visible from where the group was seated.

Charlie watched Nicole stumble down the path, her high heels certainly not made for the terrain, but gripping Jake's arm more for show than balance. She glanced back, throwing the other ladies a scandalous grin, until the two rounded a curve and disappeared from sight.

"She's such a pain in the ass," Amanda sighed when Tameka and Lori went to the restroom.

Charlie snorted, unable to argue. "If you ignore her she goes away."

Amanda shot her a 'yeah right' look. "So, looks like you and Jake are really hittin' it off."

"He's a nice guy. I like him a lot. How 'bout you?"

Amanda leaned toward her eagerly, blue eyes sparkling, her voice dropping to a conspiratorial whisper.

"Can you keep another secret?" she asked then continued before Charlie could answer. "I talked to him last night."

"Yeah? What about?"

"You."

Charlie frowned. "What? Why were you talking to Jake about me?"

Amanda shook her head, her voice enthusiastic. "Nothing bad. Only positive stuff, well for you anyway. Here's the thing. Jake and I know we don't feel anything for each other." She paused searching Charlie's face for a response.

"Go on."

"He told me I'm too young for him, and he sees me more like a little sister. I confessed that I see him more like a fun big brother," Amanda admitted with a laugh. "Crazy, right? Anyhow, I thought he'd send me home, but he said I could stay if I wanted to, since you and I are so close."

Charlie laughed, reaching again for her wineglass. "Well, that's good news for you, right?" She took another swallow and leaned back in her chair, resting the glass on her thigh.

Amanda balked at her indifference, her mouth dropping open. "You, too, Charlie! I think he really likes you."

"Ix-nay on the arlie-Chay, okay?"

"Sorry, *Char*, I think he really likes you."

"Really?"

"How'd you get through med-school?" Amanda breathed, slapping her hand to her forehead and shaking her head in exasperation. She wiped her hand down her face before saying, "You can't tell me you're missing the signals?"

Charlie thought about the interactions she and Jake had over the last three days. Of course she saw the signals, but what she didn't know is if he was sending them out to other ladies, too. "Yeah, but that's lust, y'know? Immediate attraction, hormones, and twenty different women in your house'll do that to a man."

"Maybe, but he doesn't strike me as the kind of guy who doesn't know what he wants, and I think he wants you."

Tameka and Lori returned to the table, making them cut the conversation short. Twenty minutes later Nicole came marching up the path alone, trying to wrangle the grimace on her face into a pleasurable smile. She pulled back her chair and dropped gracefully into it, crossing one leg over the other and reaching for her water. She took a deliberate swallow, the other ladies watching and waiting for her to give details.

Lori was the first to grow impatient, her heel tapping the terrace anxiously. "Well? What happened?"

"He wants to see you, Charlene," Nicole finally offered, clearly not pleased. "Said since you answered all the questions in the speed round you should get some time alone with him."

Pushing back her chair and setting her glass on the table, Charlie stood and straightened her clothes, catching Amanda's wink as she moved toward the narrow footpath. It was well tended; lined with green shrubbery and trees, and relatively smooth from being traveled. She made her way down without stumbling, and as she came to the end of the path her shoes clicked against the concrete that covered the small landing with a black wrought-iron gate surrounding the area. Jake was sitting on a wooden bench, his legs stretched out in front of him, scotch in one hand, the other arm resting across the seat back. Charlie settled near him, and he turned his head, acknowledging her arrival with a smile.

"Hey, Logan," she chirped.

"You'll notice we're alone, so don't start something you're not willing to finish," he warned, a mischievous glint in his eyes.

"Think we have enough time?" Her eyes shifted about the area quickly, and she brought her fingers up to fidget with the buttons of her shirt.

Jake narrowed his eyes a hairsbreadth. "Tease," he snickered.

Charlie laughed and dropped her hands. "Okay, I'll try to remember. I'm not much for quickies anyhow," she confided with a shrug, drawing a chuckle from Jake. She tilted back on the bench and he brought his free hand to her neck, his strong fingers gently massaging the muscles at the nape.

"Ooo, that feels good," she purred, leaning back a little more and lowering her lids. A soft breeze blew the curls of her hair, sunshine warming her face. "This is a beautiful view. How'd you find this place?"

Jake took the last swallow of his drink and rested the empty glass against his thigh. "Threw my parents an anniversary party here a couple years ago. By the way, sorry about that back there. I had no idea... about your parents."

Charlie shrugged. "It's okay. How could you know? Not exactly the type of info you put on the casting application."

His voice softened. "No... but it does mean I need to learn more about you."

"Ask away, Log—er—I mean, Jake. Whatcha wanna know?"

"What's your favorite color?" he asked, drawing her closer to him but continuing to rub her neck gently.

"Purple."

"Got any pets?"

"No. Too busy. But if I had to choose I'd get a dog. Maybe a Neapolitan or bull mastiff."

Jake threw his head back and laughed. "Why am I not surprised? Something big and powerful and mean. You don't strike me as the cutesy lapdog type."

"Heck no!" she exclaimed. "If I'm feeding it, it better be able to protect me, dammit. I don't need some tiny little thing barking like crazy while I'm being robbed. That's just addin' insult to injury!" She let their laughter subside then continued. "Come on, ask me a hard one."

"Hmm, let's see, a hard one," he started, tapping his index finger against the rim of the glass. "All right. You believe in love at first sight?"

Charlie sat up and turned to him, trying to gage the expression on his face, bringing the massage to an abrupt halt and causing his warm hand to trail down her back; the inadvertent motion sending a delicious shiver down her spine. His face was a mask, absolutely blank as if he'd just asked something mundane like "do you like orange juice?" Unable to decode his countenance, she thought on the question then answered. "No. Well...wait... let me say, not for me. I'm sure it happens, but I just don't think I'm the insta-love type." She let out a nervous little giggle then cocked her head. "Why? Do you?"

He looked out at the sea and shook his head slightly. "I didn't." Standing, he pulled her up with him, pressing her close to his chest when his arms embraced her. "Did you have a good time today?"

Her arms went around him as she looked into his eyes and smiled. "I did. Thanks, Logan."

Being so close to her and having a moment alone, Jake had to force himself not to kiss her. He'd promised he'd be on better behavior and was determined to learn more about her before things got physical. "Good," he said simply, pulling back. "But, we gotta get back to L.A."

After one last look at the view, he twined his fingers in hers and led her back up the path.

Chapter 8
{*Day 9*}

Imagine my luck! With a keen eye, and a lot of help from my teammates, we were able to win yesterday's challenge, a game of spot the fake—and no, I'm not talking about Nicole. Each team had to look through different expensive items—clothes, shoes, and jewelry—and figure out which was the real one and which was the knock-off. Amanda, Larissa, Lori, and I were able to get eight out of the ten items right and today we're going on a date as a reward. And, as team leader, I was the one who was getting extra time with Jake. I still didn't know where we were going, but I felt confident Char and I could make the switch today.

My roomies hadn't made it back to the room last night after everyone stayed up late, and were probably hung over somewhere downstairs or on the patio, so I had the space to myself. I was feeling a little anxious about leaving, but I'd already been here longer than planned. I opted to skip my morning workout and instead took a shower before all the other girls tied up the bathrooms. Dressed in a pair of tight black skinny jeans and a stylish t-shirt, I lay back down on my tiny twin bed. It was still early, and I could get all dolled up after I found out where we were going. Curled into a ball on my side, I bunched the pillow under my head and closed my eyes trying to steal a few more minutes of rest; not realizing I'd dozed into a light sleep.

I woke up with my hair in my face, a warm body pressed to my back, a big arm curved over me, and the faint scent of a dark, woodsy cologne playing in my nostrils. I sighed contentedly, nuzzling back against the warmth of what I thought was a great dream, afraid to turn over so it wouldn't end, when I heard a low

"G'mornin', angel-face." Jake's deep whisper rumbled through me making me smile as he squeezed me against his chest.

"Hey, Logan," I said softly, the first rays of sunlight burning off the coastal fog and peeking through the window. What a way to wake up!

"You looked so cute curled up in a ball I had to come lay next to you." He smoothed my wild hair back from my face and chuckled, "When was the last time you slept on a bed this small, Char?"

I smiled, imagining his long body cramped behind me on this little bed, but the cots at the hospital weren't much bigger and were far less comfortable. "It's definitely been a while. As soon as I could afford it I bought a California King and never looked back."

"Good to know I'll fit," he stated. "There's no one else sharing all that space with you, right?"

I don't think he noticed he was holding his breath and his body had tensed. I smiled again and shook my head. "No, Logan. I'm all by my onesies in there."

"Just checking," he said, dropping a kiss on my temple. "But you've gotta admit, a twin is cozy."

"Not if you plan on doing anything other than sleeping in it," I murmured.

"Yeah, well in that event a bed is completely optional," he retorted, throwing a pajama clad leg over me.

The blue and green plaid pattern caught my eye. "I figured you for an in-the-buff kind of sleeper, Logan."

"And you'd be right, Char. Didn't wanna rush you."

I was all ready with a snappy comeback when Amanda burst into the room.

"Make room for me!" She jumped on the bed, laying over us both and giggling her infectious giggle as she tried to squish us beneath her short, slender body. We became a tangle of arms, legs, and laughter as Jake tickled her mercilessly when she dropped on the bed between us.

"Okay, okay, okay!" she laughed, tears streaming down her face as she wriggled on the mattress, her arms flailing as she tried to stop him. "Stop, please! I'm really ticklish, please…" she roared. "Promise… promise, I won't do it again, please, Jake!"

Jake couldn't stop laughing himself, but finally relented his attack.

Amanda lay gasping for air next to me. "Whew! I haven't been tickled since I was a kid."

"And now I know your kryptonite," Jake winked, standing from the bed. "There's never a dull moment with you two. Be ready to go in two hours."

I sat up on the bed, running my hand through the mass of untamed curls on my head. I needed some info if Char and I were gonna switch today. "Where are we going?"

"Shopping," he said simply, turning to look at us from the door.

My eyes narrowed accusingly. "It's never that simple with you, Jake. You said lunch and flew us to Carmel. Now you say shopping. Are we gonna be local, or do I need my passport for Paris?"

He glanced at the clock then back at me with a grin. "We wouldn't make the shops before they close. Two hours, angel-face," he called as he strode out the room.

I don't know what this meant for Char and me, but I'd figure something out.

Amanda propped herself up onto an elbow, flipping her hair from her face. "Cuddling in your bed in the morning, huh? And you said you didn't see any signs. That man wants you, girl, and *bad*."

I waved the comment away and swung my feet out of bed to go finish my hair.

"Whatcha gonna wear, Char?" Amanda hopped out of the bed and yanked me by the hand, dragging me across the room. "Come on, let's look through your closet and see what you brought. I'm sure you have a bunch of cute stuff."

"I'm already dressed," I said incredulously.

Amanda gave my outfit the once-over and wrinkled her nose.

"What?" I asked looking down at my attire. The shirt was Ed Hardy, jeans by Rocawear. Finish it off with a pair of strappy heels and I was good to go. "This is trendy."

"No doubt about it, doc. It's just... look, you said it yourself. The man flew us to *Carmel* for lunch. Do you really think we're going shopping at a mall?"

I ignored her slip since no one else was around, focusing instead on her point. Chances were good she was right and we weren't just going to the mall. Still, I hate shopping, and I'd be switching with Char anyway. Why make a fuss? "Do you already know what *you're* gonna wear?"

She shook her head, practically ignoring me as she looked around the closet. "Doesn't matter if I show up in a paper bag. Jake doesn't have eyes for me. I'm the little sister type remember? You're the one whose gotta make a big impression." She rubbed her hands together before riffling through my wardrobe, going over clothes on the hangers and in my suitcases, making little 'hmm' sounds when she pulled out shoes and accessories like she was hard at work solving some great equation.

I sat back and let her take the reins. If she and Char ever met they would probably close a mall down. Nonetheless, she was doing me a big favor picking out something to wear. "Thanks, Amanda," I said, pleased to at least have made a real friend in this whole sordid mess Char had gotten me in. "This is really nice of you."

Her eyes never left the items she was holding up for appraisal; a pair of silky blue harem pants and a paisley printed blouse. "Pssh! I'm not doing this for you. If you go home, I go home," she chuckled then deadpanned, "my motivation is purely selfish."

"Yeah, well thanks anyway," I snickered, crossing my arms over my chest and leaning against the wall.

She pulled out another item and examined it over a pair of heels. "You have a lot of cute clothes. Too bad you're so tall or I'd have raided your closet already."

"Mi ropa es su ropa," I said flexing my Spanish skills. "Whatever you can fit, you're more than welcome to wear."

"Gracias! Give me a few more minutes and I'll have something cute and sassy all picked out for you."

"Perfect." I pulled myself from the wall, deciding to go make a call. "I'll be right back."

Making my way downstairs to the phones, I was careful not to wake any of the girls still sleeping. Once I was secured in the room I dialed Char's cell. It rang once then went straight to voicemail.

You've reached Charlene. I'm out of town for a few days. Leave me a message and I'll call you back! Beep!

What the... Out of town? I hung up the phone and waited a moment before picking up the receiver and dialing again. The same message played and I couldn't believe it. I talked to Char yesterday and she didn't say anything about leaving. I left her a short message anyway, just in case it was an old recording.

"Hey girl, it's me. Umm... well, we won another challenge and we're going shopping. Maybe Melrose or something, not really sure. Anyhow, call me at the house when you get this. Bye."

I returned the receiver to the cradle and exited the room. Worst case scenario, if I didn't reach her we'd have to switch another time. A wave of unease ran through me, realizing that the longer I stayed, the harder it was gonna be to leave. I tamped down the feelings and trudged up the steps, trying to convince myself that I'd get in touch with her before the date. As I entered my bedroom Amanda was returning from the closet with a pair of earrings. She laid them on the bed over the ensemble she'd picked out for me, crossing her arms as she stepped back a bit to take it all in, bobbing her head slightly with the most satisfied look on her face I'd ever seen.

"Girl, you're gonna knock him dead in this."

* * * *

I'd tried to reach Char before we left but didn't have any luck and as I sat in the stretch Hummer that was currently driving us through Beverly Hills, I figured there wasn't anything I could do but enjoy the date.

Amanda actually did a great job on the outfit, deciding on a strapless silk jumpsuit. The black one-piece had a sweetheart neckline with a twisted detail that accentuated my bust and gathered at my waist then flared into a wide leg pant that stopped at my ankles, dusting over the white gladiator sandals on my French-tipped feet—or at least that's how she explained it. Let me tell it, it was a black jumpsuit. Apart from two ringlet-curled tresses in the front, my hair had been secured with a white band into a curly ponytail on the top of my head to show off a pair of sparkling chandelier earrings. I wore a thin white gold chain around my neck, a white gold cuff on my wrist, and a trendy onyx flower ring with a Swarovski crystal center on my left hand. I even let Amanda go crazy with the makeup, doing a soft smoky eye with dabs of shimmering glitter on the inside corners and equally glistening pink lip gloss. Might as well have a little fun, right?

The car pulled to a stop on Rodeo Drive, *the* premier shopping location for people who either had lots of money to spend, or wanted to stare at the people who had lots of money to spend. Touted as the most famous shopping district in America, the three short blocks of shops and boutiques were presently flooded with a mixture of sophisticated shoppers in oversized-sunglasses, and Hawaii-shirt wearing, camera-totting tourists gawking at high-priced fashions in big bay windows. Porsche's gave way to Lamborghini's, Ferrari's to Bugatti's—the place teemed with overwhelming affluence.

ER docs make pretty good money, can't deny that. But this would be a total waste for me. You wouldn't wear Ferragamo heels while trying to stop a nosebleed or collect urine samples any more than you'd wear scrubs and clogs while shopping on Rodeo. Some things just aren't done.

I shook my head, pulling myself from unnecessary thoughts. This was Char's thing. I wouldn't have to live in it, she would. If she ended up with Logan she'd be able to shop her little heart out. And what if she did end up with Logan? I wasn't really sure if I knew how to process that possibility, and was a little detached as we piled out of the Hummer, taking in the opulence around us.

"I take it you're all familiar with Rodeo," Jake said.

I doubt the smile I was forcing actually made it up to my eyes.

"So first we're going into Juicy Couture where you have each won a head-to-toe outfit. Accessories, shoes, the works—just *try* not to bankrupt me," he added with a smile. "Then I'm gonna hang out with Char for a little one-on-one, and afterwards we'll all grab some lunch."

Lori and Larissa flanked Jake, and Amanda and I hung back a bit, linking arms as we followed them into the store.

Stepping into the boutique was like walking into a fairytale in an old-world meets rock-n-roll kind of way. The walls were colored in deep grays and various pinks with catchy sayings like 'It's exhausting to be this juicy' painted in purple. Other areas featured floor to ceiling polished pink paneling or floor length mirrors in elaborate wooden picture frames. Mannequins clad in ultra-chic clothing struck dramatic poses on throne-like chairs and ebony wood tabletops. And let's not forget the deer antlers on the wall or the gold suit of armor. Because, really, what's a fantasy without a gold suit of armor? It's a shopaholic's wet dream, effectively combining royal opulence and modern swag without being gaudy. In a word I'd say it's… juicy!

Looking around absently at the neatly displayed clothes, I tried to figure out what Char would like since she'd be the one to get more use out of the chichi threads than I would, and realized I was completely lost. I quickly gave up the battle and returned my thoughts to my dilemma with Logan.

"You okay, Char?" Amanda asked.

I shrugged, smiling weakly at her. "Just out of my element is all."

"No way. You look like you fit right in with all these über-rich people."

"Thanks to you."

"Yeah, but they're your clothes. I just picked the outfit. So what else is goin' on in that big brain of yours?" she asked, blue eyes narrowed with skepticism.

"I'm fine," I assured, because whatever it was I was feeling didn't really make any sense to me, so I certainly couldn't explain it to Amanda. I stared across the store at Jake who was laughing at something Larissa was saying, his deep timbre echoing off the polished walls and marble floors of the large boutique.

Amanda followed my gaze across the store and back to me. "You don't lie so good, doc," she said with a smile, "but I'll leave you to your thoughts. It's time to shop!"

I milled about the store, completely uninterested in anything I was looking at. Don't get me wrong the clothes were very nice. It's just I really hate shopping. And shopping with these girls is like shopping with Char; a mad dash from one item to the next. Twenty minutes in, Amanda went past me with an armload of items on her way to the dressing room.

"You haven't found anything yet," she said with mild disbelief, motioning to the clothes in her grasp with a giggle, "and I can't decide. What's wrong with this picture?"

I chuckled. "Told you, I'm out of my element. You know what, you go ahead and pick out two outfits for yourself. I don't really want anything."

She frowned uncertainly. "Serious?"

I nodded.

"Thanks, Char!" she squeaked, hugging me awkwardly over the mound of clothes in her arms before trotting into a dressing room.

I sat on a chaise lounge outside the fitting rooms. "Let me see what you're trying on since you've got enough there for a fashion show."

I heard her laughing in the cubicle when Jake came around the corner and plopped down beside me. "You always this nice?"

I shrugged. "No biggie. I have more clothes than I know what to do with." No lie there considering my necessities consisted of hospital scrubs and jeans.

"But I didn't see you even try anything on," he said, cocking a brow.

"I hate shopping," I admitted. "Give me a comfy pair of jeans, a shirt, and some sneakers and I'm golden," I smiled, once again catching my error too late. Char's a shopaholic.

Jake's face was total surprise; brown eyes roving over my outfit. "You seem to keep up with the styles. And you look absolutely great, as usual. I'd think you shop on Rodeo all the time."

"I get to keep most of the stuff from my shoots," I offered casually.

He stared at me like he was looking at an alien.

"What?" I asked suddenly self-conscious. Was there lip-gunk on my teeth?

"Smart, gorgeous, independent, knows her way around a motorcycle, *and* hates shopping?" he shook his head, crossed his fingers, and breathed, "Tell me you're a Lakers fan."

"You kiddin' me? I cut my teeth at a Lakers game! My high school jersey was number 32 like any true Magic Johnson devotee. Don't make me pull out my high tops."

"I didn't think unicorns existed," he said, his voice alight with wonder.

I flashed a smile as Amanda emerged from the dressing room in her first ensemble.

"Oh, that's looks great on you," I enthused. The girl really has a knack for fashion. Yep, she and Char would definitely enjoy going bankrupt together.

"Paired with some espadrilles, maybe," she went on excitedly, tugging at the fabric of the dress she was wearing and turning in the full-length mirror. I nodded in support in spite of the fact that I had no idea what she was talking about. She focused her attention on Jake. "What do you think?"

"Don't know what an espa-whatever is, but you look very pretty," he smiled brightly.

Amanda shook her head and walked back into the dressing room, throwing up her hands in exasperation. "Men."

I giggled as Jake grabbed my hand and pulled me from the lounge. "Hey, I'm gonna steal your audience for a while, okay?"

Amanda poked her head from the cubicle and waggled her brows at me. "Sure. You two kids have fun."

* * * *

We left Juicy Couture and strolled hand in hand a few stores down to David Yurman, a high-end jewelry store. As we entered, a well-coiffed salesman glided around a display case to greet us.

"*Monsieur* Logan," he said in French-flavored English, extending his hand. His dark eyes glittered beneath the bright store lights, warming his thin pale face. "So very nice to see you again. And who might this lovely creature be?"

"Hello, Gary," Jake replied, shaking the other man's hand firmly. "And this *'lovely creature'* is Miss Charlene Roberts. Charlene, Gary."

I extended my hand to the man and smiled. "Pleased to meet you, Gary."

He cradled my hand in both of his and began speaking softly in rapid French, thoroughly confusing me as he stared me in the eyes. "*Le plaisir est le mien, le bien-aimé. Si ceci l'un ne vous traite pas à droite—*"

"Gary," Jake warned, the faintest hint of a smile on his lips.

He released my hand then turned apologetic eyes to Jake. "*Désolé*, monsieur. What is your American term?" he asked, inclining his head as he searched the air for an answer, smiling brightly. "*Oui*, a sucker for a pretty face. Please, sit." He ushered us to a set of modern chairs at a glass-topped table. "I will bring the piece for you."

"What was that all about?" I frowned as we settled into our seats. "I didn't understand him at all."

"Just ignore Gary. He's a shameless flirt," Jake chuckled.

"Says a shameless flirt," I goaded which earned a crooked grin.

"*Touché.*"

"Do you know what he said?"

He angled toward me and looked at me thoughtfully. "I believe it was 'the pleasure is all mine, sweetheart, and if he doesn't treat you right...' That's where I stopped him, because Gary's notorious for innuendo that would *not* amuse me where you're concerned."

A smile quirked my lips as a woman arrived with flutes of champagne on a tray, offering them to us before retreating to wherever she materialized from.

"The royal treatment," I said, sipping the bubbling liquid. "Is this how you always shop, Logan?"

He shook his head. "I hate shopping, too, which is why I have a stylist. Gotta stay sharp for public appearances, but I'd rather be in a pair of jeans right along with you, angel-face. I endure it only when I have to."

"So what are you here for today?"

He motioned with his glass as Gary arrived with two padded black velvet lined cases. He set them on the tabletop and took a seat opposite us, pulling on a pair of cloth gloves. Opening the first tray with great care, he removed a large watch as he went into a brisk, business-like dialogue about the specifications of the piece, delivering it to Jake with white-glove hands.

"I present to you the *Belmont*. Swiss automatic chronograph; thirty-seven jewels; water resistant to thirty-point-four-eight meters. Stainless steel case with domed scratch-resistant sapphire crystal face and exhibition back. The dial is black galvanic guilloche with silver indexes and white hands."

Jake examined the watch thoroughly then placed it on his wrist, fumbling to connect the two ends. Without a second thought I settled my flute on the table and helped him.

"Thanks, baby," he smiled, as I secured the clasp and Gary continued his speech.

"The signature Yurman Cabled bracelet is also of stainless steel. Retail price on it is—"

"Not necessary," Jake interrupted, holding his hand up to stop the disclosure. "Whatcha think, Char?"

I grabbed his arm, turning his wrist this way and that, really appraising the piece, and taking the opportunity to feel his hands. He has really strong hands, not too rough, warm, with long fingers—capable hands. Hands that would feel so good gliding down my body, it made me shiver thinking about it. But, getting back to the watch, it was definitely nice, reflecting Jake's elegant style without being too stuffy. It looked great on him. "I think it's you, Logan."

"Perfect. I'll take it. In fact, Gary, I'll wear it out."

"*Oui, monsieur*. Would you like to see the second tray? Something, perhaps, for *Mademoiselle* Roberts?"

Glancing at Jake with a surprised frown, I shook my head and waved both hands vigorously. "Oh, no thank you, Gary. We were just here to get Logan's watch."

"Well let's *at least* see what he's brought," Jake enthused, to which Gary beamed and opened the second case.

He reached in and removed the item, reverently holding it between two gloved fingers. "May I present the *Cross Over Cable Pavé Engagement Ring.* The piece—"

"Engagement ring!" I squeaked, interrupting his narrative. "Moving a little fast there, aren't we Gary?"

Jake feigned hurt, making a sad little puppy dog face with a full on pout. It was the cutest damn thing I'd ever seen. "Is that a 'no', Char?"

"You're not helping matters, Logan." My throat went dry and my heart started to race. I reached for my champagne and inelegantly downed the rest of the glass, hoping like hell it would give me a buzz. Unfortunately it didn't, and I took a deep breath trying to settle my unfounded nerves.

"Just try it on," came his encouraging retort with a chuckle.

I shook my head. Call me superstitious, but I'd done this once before, trying the ring on *before* I'd been proposed to, y'know, to be prepared and all. Well that didn't exactly work out so great. In fact, to be completely honest, he never got around to asking me. No sense in tempting the fates twice, right?

Jake draped his arm around my chair, leaning towards me as he dropped his voice to a silky whisper. "If it helps, Gary does this whenever I come into the store with someone. I think he likes the shock value. Last time I was here he pulled the same trick." His eyes slid to the quiet salesman who was observing our entire conversation with an innocent smile.

That comment rippled through me. Surprisingly, it bothered me. To think of Logan coming into this store—

or *any* store for that matter—and shopping with some other woman actually had my stomach in knots.

"And just who were you here with last, huh, Logan?" I asked, cocking a brow and trying to keep the smile on my face and the grimace off it.

"Easy, angel-face," he said, picking up on my unspoken fears. He pulled his arm from around me and took my hand removing the flower ring, placing it gently on the table. "It was my mother and a diamond necklace. So try it on, just to see how it looks, okay?" He took the ring from Gary who began his discourse on the piece.

"*Oui.* The ring features a Yurman Signature Cut diamond in a white gold setting. The focal diamond is two-point-six-seven carats, certified colorless and flawless. A total of thirty-six pavé diamonds surround it—nine on each arm of the bands, each no less than point-two-five carats. And note how both cabled bands cross each other on the diagonal, as if woven together. That is to represent the joining of the two hearts as one," he said wistfully then returned to his business-like clip, "retail price—"

"Is, again, not necessary," Jake admonished as he slid the ring onto my finger.

Maybe it was the situation. Or maybe it was the feel of his fingertips lightly holding my hand and grazing my skin as he seated the ring on my finger, but a jolt of electricity raced through me, leaving me breathless. I felt his gaze on my face, but couldn't look at him for fear my eyes would reveal too much.

"Fits perfectly, Char," he said softly.

"It's beautiful," I breathed, holding my hand up to admire it. The light caught the diamond expertly, the pristine sparkle refracting on my skin and clothing. I rubbed my thumb against the underside of the bands, reminded of that silly fairytale Charlene and I grew up on about how we got our eyes. The way the bands were twisted vaguely resembled how I'd pictured the rings my ancestor wove for her secret marriage to Igrár. I looked up to catch Jake smiling at me.

"Am I gonna have a hard time getting that off you?" he smirked. "Or should I just marry you already?"

Ignoring his comments, and the thudding of my heart, I plucked the ring from my finger, casually handing it over. "Here you are, Gary. It really is gorgeous."

"As is its wearer," the man complimented, cleaning the ring with a cloth and returning it to its case.

Jake slid my own ring back on my finger.

"You just practicing, Logan?" I asked, trying to shake off whatever this feeling was.

He flashed me a grin then turned his attention to the salesman.

"Just the watch then, monsieur?"

Jake nodded removing his wallet from his pocket. "For now, Gary, thank you." He plucked a credit card from the leather pouch and placed it on the table.

"I shall prepare your bill." Gary gathered the card and two cases and glided away.

I reached for my champagne, fingers slightly trembling, and, realizing the flute was empty, reached for Jake's. In a repeat performance, I downed his glass and set it on the table. That entire experience was unnerving as hell and I needed something to help calm my jitters.

"You okay, angel-face?" Jake asked grasping my hand and twining our fingers, an action I'd actually come to expect and enjoy.

"Never better, Logan," I chirped. Gary returned with the receipt and a small handle bag with the watch box stowed inside. He handed it to me as if I were the one who made the purchase.

Jake brought our joined hands to the table, bracing the slip of paper as he signed the receipt and then holding his wallet as he slipped his credit card back into its proper slot.

"Didn't want to let you go," he smiled, returning the billfold to his pocket when we stood. "An experience as always, Gary," he called over his shoulder, leading me to the door.

"*Oui, Monsieur* Logan. Please visit us again soon. Perhaps next time the ring for *Mademoiselle* Roberts," Gary said, inclining his head slightly and clasping his hands behind his back.

Yeah right, I thought, but smiled politely as we went out the door.

Chapter 9
{Day 22}

Having lost yet another challenge a couple days before—that one involving copious amounts of chocolate pudding, an inflatable swimming pool, and bikinis—Charlie was beginning to worry. It had been nearly two weeks since her last date with Jake, which meant time was quickly slipping away and she desperately needed to make the switch with Char, whose only excuse for being unavailable for the last date was that she "needed to get away".

Standing in the bathroom, Charlie leaned against the countertop and stared into the mirror, diligently working the floss between her teeth, trying to remove a stuck popcorn kernel, when the door flew open and slammed shut in almost the same instant. Wide-eyed, she looked at her visitor, the floss still in her teeth and mouth agape.

"Sorry to interrupt you. Flossing? Excellent. Gotta take care of that beautiful smile, angel-face," Jake said glancing at her briefly before quickly looking around. She watched in the mirror while he pulled open the door to the linen closet, shook his head, and then strode to the window. He groaned as though he'd just remembered they were three stories up, then made a beeline to the shower, stepped in, and drew the frosted glass door shut.

What the hell was that about? Charlie wondered when the bathroom door flew open again. A bubbly brunette with her cleavage spilling out of her top poked her head in. Charlie resumed her flossing, trying hard to suppress a smile.

"Did Jake-y come in here?" Tabitha whined in that annoying baby voice that made Charlie want to choke her.

Charlie frowned and shook her head. "Nope. Just me and my floss."

Tabitha pouted and stomped her foot. "I *swear* he is the *hardest* man to *find* around here. Well if you see him, let him know I'm looking for him, 'kay?"

"Sure thing," Charlie replied, returning her full attention to her teeth.

Tabitha turned on her heel and shut the door behind her. Thirty seconds later Jake emerged from the shower looking relieved.

"I owe you one, Charlene," he exhaled, scrubbing his hand over his head. "That girl just doesn't know when to quit. Now how the hell am I gonna get out of here? Don't get me wrong, I'm always glad to be in your company, but I don't plan on spending the evening locked in the bathroom."

Charlie finished with the floss, washed her hands, and turned to Jake.

God he's sexy, she thought, watching the way his muscles bunched beneath his t-shirt as he shoved his hands in the pockets of his pants. *And he smells so good, like something spicy and enticing yet still subtle.*

"Any ideas?" His eyes slowly roved over her body.

Beneath his glare she realized she was less than formally attired, wearing only a pink camisole—sans a bra—and black lace panties. In fact, her most fully covered body parts were her feet, which were swathed in comfy black house slippers. Her nipples hardened and she felt a heat flush through her. Jake noticed her discomfort and grinned, then looked around, reconsidering the window.

"Unless you sprout wings in the next ten seconds I'd say that's not an option," she said casually moving to the door, her voice much cooler than she felt. "I'll make sure it's clear then you can get back to your room."

He shook his head. "Uh-uhn. Can't go back there. Not yet, anyhow. Tabitha and the rest of her crew are waiting. I need a break from all that for a while and they just don't seem to comprehend 'can you give me a minute' regardless of the language it's said in. I've tried English, Spanish, French...English with a British accent *and* an Australian accent," he said sarcastically. "I'd try Farsi if I thought that would help,"

"Okay, your room's not an option." Charlie chuckled, thinking it over. Then it struck her. She knew exactly where she'd take him. "Be back for you in a sec."

She exited the bathroom and entered the bedroom and, finding it empty, figured her remaining two roommates were probably downstairs at the bar or passed out on the couches. She wriggled into a pair of black sweats and matching sweatshirt, slid her feet into a pair of sneakers, then left the bedroom and turned right, opening the first door she came to. She peeked in quickly to make sure it was empty as usual.

The study held floor-to-ceiling bookshelves finished in a beautiful maple wood stuffed with books on a multitude of topics. Most of the girls hadn't bothered to venture into the pristine space, probably because the door was always closed keeping that sweet, musty, old book smell trapped inside. But it was one of the reasons Charlie chose the bedroom she was in. It had no cameras—presumably because sexy girls reading books did not boost ratings—and she could come and read without being interrupted by the craziness and drama that happened in the house.

In the center of the room a maple wood desk sat empty, a dainty reading lamp off to the corner. There was also a plush leather couch as well as a comfy desk chair, both perfect for curling up in. But the best feature of the room wasn't immediately obvious. In fact, she'd only noticed it the last time she'd come in. Above the desk was a panel, and that was where she'd tell Jake he could hide out for a while.

Returning to the bathroom to retrieve her fugitive, she quickly led Jake back into the study, careful not to make too much noise since his bedroom was directly across from it; the double doors wide open and Tabitha and friends lounging across his bed and divan knee-deep in their usual gossip. They entered the study and Charlie silently closed the door behind them, flipping on the overhead light.

Jake looked around skeptically. "I don't think this is gonna last too long."

Charlie simply lifted her hand, pointing her index finger up.

When Jake saw the panel a grin lit his face. "Know where it goes?"

"To the roof. You can hang out in the *girl-free* zone until they either leave or pass out," she joked then murmured, "but my money's on them passing out first." She hopped onto the desk and pulled the panel down. A short set of stairs emerged from the door, revealing another panel at the top.

"Well haven't you been busy," he said. "Any other secret passages in this house?"

"Don't know. Haven't had to look yet."

Jake helped her off the desk before climbing up. He cramped his long body onto the stairs and grumbled, "Damn, this is tight."

"Yeah, well, for season two you can request a custom-built escape chute," she mocked. "It's all I can come up with at the moment, so get a move on, Logan. I'll come back for you in a couple hours."

"You're not coming?" he frowned, stopping halfway up the short ladder and looking down at her.

Her heart beat a little faster but she managed a casual, "I thought you needed some space from the fairer sex."

His gaze softened. "I *want* you to come, Charlene."

Every time he said Char's name it reminded Charlie that she wasn't supposed to be here. It was Charlene whose career this would benefit, and Charlene who would be here just as soon as they could make the switch. It would be foolish to continue tempting herself with Jake Logan, because after the next few days, *she* would never see him again. Char would.

"Of course, I'm coming," she smiled back. "Be up in a minute."

As soon as he was gone Charlie shut off the lights in the study and went to Jake's room, met by the eager stares of Tabitha and the four other girls she hung out with.

"Find him?" Tabitha chirped.

"No. I thought maybe he'd come back here," Charlie said filling her voice with disappointment as she casually crossed the room. "I saw a sweatshirt I wanted to ask him about, so I'll just grab it in case I see him."

The four girls went back to their super-deep conversation about the latest celebrity baby and Charlie went to Jake's walk-in closet. The space was immaculate; clothes hung on hangers, folded and placed neatly on shelves, shoes organized, belts and accessories in cubbies. She admired the fact that it was so clean, because the ladies in the house had items of clothing spilling from every location *but* the closet and bureaus. Returning her attention to the task at hand, she rifled through his wardrobe trying to find anything warm. It may be a summer's evening in Los Angeles, but being this close to the beach the roof would feel like a winter's day in Jersey. She pulled a thick blue zippered hoodie from a hanger and threw it on over her own sweatshirt. It hung off of her, making her look like a girl playing dress up in her parent's clothing. It smelled like Jake and she inhaled deeply, drawing the fabric tightly around her. She let herself imagine dating him, *really* dating him, for just a second before she returned to her senses, left the closet, and walked briskly out the room.

Once on the roof she saw Jake staring out at the unhindered view of the Pacific Ocean. Even from this distance she could just make out the whitecaps of the waves as they crashed to the shore in the waning sunlight.

"Nice view, huh?"

She nodded, shrugging out of his coat. "Gets a little cold up here," she said, handing it to him, reluctant to have his scent leave her. Charlie took a seat on the curved red concrete tiles and continued to stare at the water.

"Thanks." Jake slid his arms into the sleeves but left the jacket open. "How long have you been coming up here?" he asked, settling close to her and leaning back onto his hands, stretching his legs out before him.

"Just once before. It gets really cramped in that room," she explained, trying to slow the flutters in her belly as their legs brushed and he made no move to adjust them. "So I started going into the study, because the other girls never go in there. I just noticed that panel a few days ago and decided to do a little exploring." Charlie turned and pointed behind him. "If you go that way the roof drops off and you're on your balcony."

"Ahh, so you're the one who's been sneaking into my room late night," he joked.

She shook her head and smiled. "Scout's honor, no peeping. Just exploring."

"Well, I'm glad you did. This is a nice change of pace. No drama and no cameras." He bounced his foot absently. "I miss you."

Charlie frowned at him, an ironic smile on her face. "We're living in the same house, Jake."

"I know," he said, shaking his head. "I just mean… we haven't hung out in a while, have we, angel-face?"

Charlie grunted. "Cause I keep ending up on horrible teams. Makes it hard to win dates. Plus the girls are always badgering you for time and attention. I figured you might like a little breathing room."

"Am I that transparent?" he chuckled, nudging her with his knee. "Well, I like spending time with you, so don't be a stranger."

She nodded, turning her gaze back to the ocean. After they sat in silence for a stretch she finally spoke again.

"Why are you here, Logan?"

He raised a brow as she shifted her body enough to look at him fully.

"I mean," she chewed her bottom lip, "a guy like you doesn't need to do a show like this to get a woman. Yeah you're in the spotlight, but you seem to be a pretty private person, so it doesn't fit that you'd want to do a reality show about your love life. *Clearly* you don't like clingy girls—exhibits A through E being Tabitha and friends. I noticed you haven't really kissed anyone, maybe a peck on the cheek or something, but you don't really seem to be all gung ho about getting physical…" She trailed off at the smirk he gave her then continued matter-of-factly, "you know what I mean. Sure you flirt—that's the nature of the beast—but you don't really seem interested in having a fling. And I don't think you're here for publicity. *Soooo…*"

Jake stared at her stone-faced thinking, *if only you knew.* Charlene was definitely observant, which was one of the reasons he was so drawn to her. There was something different about her, a depth the other girls lacked. But she seemed to have missed what he figured was the most obvious.

"Sorry," she said quickly, misreading his expression. "Am I getting too personal?"

Jake relented with a grin. "It's okay, angel-face. That's what the show's all about, right? Getting up-close-and-personal with bad boy Jake Logan."

"'Bad boy'?" she snorted. "Hardly. I might have thought that before I got here, but anyone who's been around you can tell you're a big softie."

Crap! she thought. She hadn't meant to say that. Celebrities were all about their reputations. She searched his face to see if he knew she was joking, but his dark brown eyes didn't reveal a trace of what he was thinking.

He let out a soft chuckle and shook his head. Marcus had said the exact same thing. How was it possible that Charlene, who'd met him roughly three weeks ago, could know him so well?

"Damn, there goes my rep." He held a finger to his lips, his eyes twinkling. "Don't tell the tabloids, okay? Our secret."

"Sorry," she demurred. "Foot-in-mouth disorder. I sometimes speak before I think."

"Don't be. That's one of the things I like about you. You're very honest. Most women I've dated are as plastic as the dolls they're pretending to be. They agree with everything I say or make sure they always say or do the right thing. They do everything but be who they are. With you there's no pretense, no bullshit. I appreciate it, Charlene."

There was that name, again. *This is becoming a problem,* Charlie thought. She pushed the feelings away deciding to steal this moment for herself. After all, this may be the last moment she got.

"You're funny and you're smart," he continued. "It's like you're here competing, but you're not just trying to win the game. Does that make sense?"

She nodded.

"And there's something about you I can't put my finger on. Something... mysterious." He sat forward, brushing his hands on his pants, the movement bringing his face closer to hers.

Charlie licked her lips then offered casually, "It's the eyes. Gray eyes seem to always hold a secret."

"Your eyes may have drawn me in, but your mind makes me want to stay." He gently caressed her cheek and outlined her lower lip with the pad of his thumb. "All around you're gorgeous, angel-face." He stared at her a beat before returned his hands behind him and leaning back, stopping himself before he went too far.

Charlie let out a shaky breath, her heart pounding in her chest so hard she just knew he could hear it. She wanted him. God, did she want him! All the alarms were flashing and the warning bells were ringing. Getting any closer to Jake Logan would be completely devastating for her. She turned her head and watched the distant red and white lights of the cars as they snaked up Pacific Coast Highway.

The sky had turned a marbled purple/magenta/pink color, and the sun would be down in a few short minutes. Then it would really get cold. She drew her knees to her chest and wrapped her arms tightly about them. Having gotten out of the shower only a short time before, her body was starting to feel the chill. Jake noticed her shivering and scooted behind her so that she sat between his long legs. Then he enfolded her in his arms, pressing her back against his chest in an attempt to warm her.

He spoke softly in her ear as they both looked out at the ocean in the distance. "My life is one event after the next. It's always go, go, go. You ever feel like that?" Charlie nodded, snuggling back into him and closing her eyes, loving the feel of his strong arms around her shielding her from the cold. "The ER is always like that," she sighed. "Constantly on the move from one crisis to the next."

"ER?"

She stiffened, noticing her fumble. *Dammit Charlie*, she admonished silently, *you're getting too comfortable.* "Uh, yeah. That's what I call it when I'm on a shoot. Photographers act like everything is the emergency room, you know. Life or death situations. We're not saving lives here; it's just a picture. "

He chuckled and she could feel his warm laugh reverberate in her own chest. She relaxed against him again before continuing. "But every now and then I make sure to take a moment to slow down."

"If I slow down I feel like I might miss something."

"Yeah, but if you didn't slow down today, you'd have missed that," she murmured, pointing to the sun as the last rays slipped below the horizon. "You would have missed everything, Logan."

At the throaty sound of his name, Jake bent his head and pressed soft kisses on her neck then gently nipped her earlobe. He ran his hands down her sides, outlining her slender torso beneath the baggy sweatshirt. Charlie arched against him, warmth racing through her body in response to his touch. She turned to face him, kneeling between his outstretched legs, and found his eyes mirrored her own.

Smoldering heat.

He wanted her as much as she wanted him. And even though those alarms in her head were blaring now, she ignored them.

Heartbreak be damned.

He kissed her fully on the lips, his tongue searching her mouth, savoring the taste of her as he pulled her body to his. She felt so right touching him, wrapping her arms about his neck as he slid his hands lower to squeeze her curved bottom, and back up and under the thick fabric of her sweatshirt to caress the soft skin of her lower back. She moaned softly as he lightly sucked her lower lip. Unable to get any closer he tugged the sweatshirt over her head and tossed it aside. She inhaled sharply as the cool air hit her.

Jake marveled at the sight of the full globes of her breasts pressed tautly against her thin tank top, the stiff peaks tugging at the material. "You really are beautiful, angel-face," he said hoarsely.

Charlie shivered as his mouth grazed a nipple through the fabric, his hot breath causing it to harden in response even more than the cold air. She felt the tingle of anticipation building low in her belly. In one swift move Jake had the tank top off, Charlie on her back, and was lying between her splayed legs. She could feel the firm bulk of his growing erection through her sweatpants, and the realization made her breath quicken.

Jake leisurely kissed her lips again, then the hollow of her neck; licking a trail of fire everywhere he felt her pulse pounding. He brushed his lips along her collarbone and down her dark, supple breast, drawing one firm tip into his mouth and biting down gently, flicking his tongue across it.

"Oh, god, Jake," Charlie whimpered, feeling the dampness begin between her thighs. She ran her hands over his short-cropped hair as his tongue trailed down her body, kissing and nipping the soft roundness of her belly. He inched her sweatpants down, licking the curve of an exposed hip.

"I've been thinking about you like this since I first saw you," he murmured thickly between caresses. "You've been in my dreams so long I can't believe I really have you here, Char."

The trip back to reality was swift, the fiery gaze leaving Charlie's eyes almost the instant he'd mentioned her sister's name.

She couldn't do this.

She *wanted* to do this.

Hell, right now she *needed* to do this.

But she couldn't.

Jake noticed her stiffen, looking up to study her face and seeing the change in her expression. "Oh, damn, I'm s—I'm sorry," he stammered, pulling himself off her abruptly and retrieving her clothes. "I didn't mean for this to happen—no, that's a lie. I *did* mean for this to happen, just not like—like this."

Charlie sat up staring blankly out into space; a chill swiftly pervading every part of her and it wasn't from the cold night air. There was a profound sense of loss without him holding her, touching her, but the deeper pain came from realizing the ramifications of her deception. Jake Logan would never know Charlie for who she truly was.

Detached, she felt him draw the tank over head and slide her arms in the thin straps, followed by her sweatshirt. Then he pulled her to her feet and hugged her tightly, rubbing his hands up and down her back briskly trying to warm her, and enjoying the feel of her, the smell of her, the remembered taste of her. Then he forced his hands to his sides.

"I'm a real ass. You deserve so much more than a concrete rooftop, baby," he grimaced, rubbing a hand over his head. "But if you don't leave from here soon, I can't promise you'll get it." He cupped her face in his hands and kissed her deeply again, thinking about how he'd almost backed out of doing the show and how he would have never met the beautiful woman standing before him. "You're right, you know? I almost missed everything." He slowly backed in the opposite direction of the study, needing to put space between them but unable to resist watching her shapely body as she left him. "Good night, angel-face."

She frowned. "You're not coming?"

"I think I need to cool off a bit before going back down there. I'll go to the other side and drop onto the balcony later."

Charlie willed her legs to carry her the short distance across the roof to the access panel, fighting a sudden welling of tears in her eyes. It was stupid to get this emotional, and over what? Feelings caused by a moment of lust? *Just hormones, Charlie*, she tried to convince herself. But she suddenly felt extremely lonely, conflicted, and… something else. Something she wasn't able to describe or willing to admit.

"Hey," Jake called after her, surprising her by how close his voice sounded.

Charlie blinked back the tears and turned to face him, forcing a light smile onto her face. She hadn't put as much space between them as she'd thought.

"About the show," he said, shoving his hands into his pants pockets, "why I'm doing it."

She nodded, prompting him to go on.

"I found my reason."

Chapter 10
{*Day 24*}

It had been just over three weeks that I'd been in the house, and there were only twelve of us left. Having not won a date since our shopping trip to Rodeo, Char and I hadn't been able to switch. But after a win today at the basketball challenge I got the news that us winners— Amanda, Nicole, and myself—would be partying in VIP tonight with Jake at his club in Hollywood.

I went to the phone and dialed Char's number. I'd called her almost daily to give her updates so she'd know who was who and what was what when she got here, but I didn't get a chance to talk to her about the events of the other night, deciding it was safer to tell her in person.

She finally answered on the fifth ring.

"Hello, Charlene," Char said cheerfully.

"Hey, girl," I replied keeping an eye on the door and remembering that the phone calls were taped.

"How's everything going?"

I sighed heavily. "Honestly, it's getting complicated."

"With the other girls?"

"Negative."

"I see. Care to explain?"

I considered it for a moment. I knew I was here for Char and her career, but somewhere along the way I started being here for me—and for Jake. I didn't know how to tell Char because I wasn't really sure what it was I wanted, or I wasn't ready to *admit* what it was I wanted. I didn't know which. If I didn't switch, Char would be devastated. On the other hand if I did, I'd lose any chance of being with Jake.

"Nothing to explain. So we won today," I said excitedly, changing the subject and getting down to business. "Tonight Amanda, Nicole, and I are gonna go to

Jake's club in Hollywood, the Red Room. VIP booth of course! It's always so hard to get in there."

"Oh! I know a couple bouncers there. Maybe I'll run into you and you could introduce me to this Jake guy you're so crazy about," she said, dropping into the act.

She'd hit the nail on the head and didn't know it. I giggled anxiously. "Yeah, that *would* be interesting."

"You already know what you're gonna wear?" she continued.

"Uh-uhn. Any suggestions?"

"I think the magenta mini with the thigh-high suede black boots."

I groaned inwardly. Even "mini" made the dress sound much longer than it was. "Micro" bordering on "nano" was more like it. The dress was so short that if I wanted to cover my ass, I'd have to pull up the boots! Still, I knew Char had a similar dress at home by a different designer, so wearing almost matching magenta minis would be easier than trying to change in a crowded nightclub bathroom.

"How should I do my hair?"

"Umm... I'm thinking big, loose ringlets all over your head. But nothing major on the makeup, the dress will speak for itself."

I heard Jake calling for all the girls to join him in the living room and had to cut the conversation short.

"Great advice, as always! Anyhow, they're calling for us so I gotta run. Talk to you soon."

We said our goodbyes and, feeling somewhat somber I went into the living room to spend the last few hours I had with Logan.

* * * *

Jake was standing in the living room with all the girls when Charlie entered.

A faint smile played on her lips as she watched him interact with everyone, making each girl feel as though she had his undivided attention in spite of the fact that they were all talking. She really liked that about him. Who was she kidding? She liked *everything* about him.

Jake smiled as she joined the group.

"And Charlene makes twelve," he said, turning to the glass table and lifting a tented card. "The producers left this here for me and said I had to read it out loud for everyone, so we're all getting the news at the same time."

He unfolded the note and read the text with a frown. "Sometimes a blast from your past can influence your future."

"Does that mean you're meeting our ex-boyfriends or something?" Larisa asked. "'Cause that's probably not the best thing. I can't *stand* my ex."

Several girls agreed, shaking their heads at the very notion of being in the same room with their former lovers, some actually mentioning restraining orders and police reports.

The doorbell rang and moments later the front door swung open, drawing everyone's attention toward it. In the doorway stood yet another gorgeous woman, her five-foot-nine frame draped in a short colorful summer dress. Jet-black hair was pulled back into a chignon with a flower tucked over one ear, and oversized shades covered her honey-colored face.

"Hello, Jake," she said in a tone that dripped familiarity with a hint of seduction.

Everyone paused, most watching the woman, but Charlie and a few others watching Jake. His expression was a mixture of utter surprise and absolute anger.

"AJ, we need to talk," he said, straining for calm. "*Now.*"

He crumbled the note and tossed it on the floor, marching over to the producer and grasping her by the elbow. He led AJ to an adjoining room and deliberately shut the door.

The remaining girls chatted amongst themselves, whispering about their visitor. Charlie went into the kitchen and returned with a bottle of water, taking a seat on a nearby divan, watching as the newcomer stepped over the threshold and appraised each woman in the house. When the woman looked in her direction Charlie smiled but got nothing for her effort.

Minutes later Jake and AJ emerged from the room. Jake forced a smile as he went to the door and greeted the woman with a quick hug and a peck on the cheek as though the incident before had never happened.

"I'm sure you all know my ex, Tamara James. She's dropped by to give me her opinion of you ladies and to let you all know more about me, so she's gonna hang out with you a little while today. She'll also be joining us at the club tonight, if that's all right with Amanda, Nicole, and Charlene."

"Sure," Charlie piped, taking another swallow of water. The borrowed time she'd been on was officially up. As of tonight she'd be getting back to her life and whatever happened in this nuthouse would be Char's problem.

Jake continued stiffly. "Great. I'll leave you all to it." He climbed the stairs and didn't look back.

The tension in the room was palpable and no one said a word for a time until finally Tamara spoke, raising the sunglasses to rest on her head.

"Well, let's all go get a drink and talk a while, okay?"

Eleven women followed Tamara out to the patio eager to ask her the questions they'd all undoubtedly had about her relationship with Jake and their newsworthy break-up. Charlie, however, climbed the stairs, determined to spend her last few hours with the man, not his ex. She rapped lightly on the door to the master suite.

"Yeah," came Jake's terse reply. "S'open."

She entered and gently closed the door behind her, watching Jake who stood across the room at the door to his balcony observing all the women around the bar chatting and laughing with his ex.

Charlie sank onto a plush loveseat against the wall and draped a long leg over the arm. "Not your favorite person, huh?" she asked lightly.

He spun to face her and smiled. "I kinda figured it was you," he said, walking back into the room and taking a seat on his bed. "Tamara doesn't bother me."

"No bullshit and no pretense. Isn't that what you said, Logan?"

Jake grinned, caught in the lie. "You're right, my bad. Truth is if I never saw her again it'd be too soon."

"Why's that? Apart from her dumping you, of course."

He didn't respond and she held up her hands in apology. "If you don't wanna talk about it that's fine. I won't push."

"You ever been in love, Char? I mean *really* in love?"

She thought about it. There was one guy about four years ago named Kadir, and Charlie loved him madly. They'd begun their residencies together and had dated almost a year. They were as inseparable as two overworked underpaid potential physicians could be, spending every available second together. But eventually they were put on different shifts, leaving little time for them to see each other away from the hospital. Nonetheless, Charlie thought Kadir loved her as much as she did him, and that one day he'd propose. That is, until she walked in on him playing 'doctor' with his head nurse, learning later that he'd been unfaithful their entire relationship.

"Do you miss him?" Jake asked uncertainly, misinterpreting the look on her face.

Charlie shook her head forcefully and couldn't hide the revulsion in her voice. "God no! Not in the least. The man cheated on me the whole time we were together and I didn't figure it out until I caught him. It's been four years since and sometimes I still wonder why I loved him in the first place. And I don't think he ever loved me, not if he cheated the whole time. So, no, I don't think I've ever really been in love, 'cause when you are, you're supposed to get loved back, right?"

He exhaled the breath he was holding and bobbed his head. "Now you get what I'm saying. Although I'd like to personally thank the man who let you go."

Charlie studied him a moment with a frown as understanding dawned. "So the papers had it wrong? Tamara cheated on *you*?"

He nodded solemnly, shifting his shoulders. "Like I said, angel-face, committed a hundred percent. Not one of my exes can honestly say I've cheated on her because I never have. Look, in my line of work I talk to a lot of people, especially women. I admit to being a flirt only because I have to make sure people are having a great time at my clubs, and the photogs are always there to snap a picture or two with me and some girl I don't know. The next day, she's the latest notch in my bedpost, according to the glossies.

"I loved Tamara, and it took me three years to realize she didn't feel the same for me. The woman's a leach whose sole purpose in life is to get ahead. I think I saw what I wanted to see instead of what was really there, y'know? Anyhow, I eventually broke off our engagement—quietly. To save face, she goes to the press with some story about *me* cheating on her. The following day our break-up is front-page news. A week later she's with some new hotshot movie producer and her previously nonexistent acting career is blooming."

Charlie saw the torment in his eyes and felt the urge to march down the stairs and pummel the woman who'd put it there. She swallowed hard, tamping down an unexplained case of nerves and asked cautiously, "Do you still love her?"

He was opening his mouth to answer when his bedroom door pushed open.

"There you are, Jake!" Tamara exclaimed, entering the room with a glass of wine in one hand and a tumbler of scotch in the other. Nicole, Tabitha, and two other girls filed in behind her, flanking him on all sides on his bed.

"You feeling okay, baby?" Nicole asked, kneeling behind him and massaging his shoulders, crushing the back of his head to her breasts.

"Couldn't be better."

"So," Tamara said, sliding her petite frame onto Jake's lap and smiling wickedly as she pressed the glass into his hand. "You must be Charlene. The other girls tell me you're the current apple of Jake's eye."

Charlie couldn't help but notice his free hand had come to rest around the woman's waist; the move so automatic it had been burned into his subconscious. And his eyes had closed as though he were thoroughly enjoying the massage Nicole was giving him.

"Oh, I wouldn't say that," she replied caustically, unable to mask the twinge of irritation in her voice. Jake's eyes flew open as she continued, "In fact, I think there are several women here Jake's interested in." Charlie forced a giggle. "That's why we're all here, though. We all wanna see him happy no matter who he chooses. Right, Logan?"

He stared back at ice-gray eyes, continuing his silence, but Tamara noticed the unspoken words passing between them.

"*Logan*? Is that what you call him? How…cute," she said in a condescending tone then, lowering her voice seductively, "I won't tell them what I call you, Jake." She let that hang in the air a beat then turned back to Charlie. "Nicole said you're a model. Print or runway?"

Charlie shifted her gaze a quarter-inch to eye the woman perched on Jake's lap. "Both."

"I did some modeling before my acting career took off. I was even Givenchy's muse for a while, remember, Jake? Have you worked with any major designers?"

Charlie accepted the challenge. "Actually I just finished a D&G shoot, and I've also done Sean John, Rocawear, and Olivier Strelli to name a few."

"I didn't know that," Jake said, lifting the tumbler to his lips.

"Because they're jobs, they're not me," Charlie shrugged. "Knowing me doesn't have a thing to do with who I work for." It was a loaded statement, but he didn't know it. She sat back and watched the other five women crowding Jake, especially Tamara who had snuggled close to her former fiancé. She couldn't help but feel that, while it might hurt, leaving tonight would be for the best.

"So you plan to get into acting later?" Tamara asked.

"No."

"You should consider it, sweetie," she continued in her patronizing tone. "She's got a lovely face, don't you agree, Jake?"

Jake took a moment looking over the gorgeous woman across from him, understanding that Tamara had chosen her as the sacrificial lamb. Too quick to agree and the other girls would gang up on her. Too passive and she might think he wasn't interested, when truth be told she was the only woman he wanted. He chose a casual but confident reply, staring deep into her gray eyes. "Char knows how I feel about her."

Tamara's head swiveled from Charlie to Jake and back again, a wicked grin on her face. "Hmmph. I'm sure she does." She took a swallow of her wine and rose from Jake's lap. "Well, I'm going to talk with the other ladies and see what they're all about. What club are we going to, babe?"

The endearment wasn't lost on Charlie who was forcing herself to remain seated.

"The Red Room," Jake replied clearing his throat. "We'll leave in a couple hours."

"Ooh, the Red Room. Have you ever been there, Charlene? It's a-*mazing*! Remember what we did after closing that night, Tank?" Tamara asked, winking at Jake and running a hand suggestively up his thigh. "Good times. See you later."

She swept out the door with the other girls on her heels, leaving Charlie and Jake alone once again.

"Tank?" Charlie raised a brow.

He shrugged, grinning mischievously. "I was fascinated with the army as a kid."

Charlie shook her head and chuckled. "I sincerely doubt that's why she calls you that."

* * * *

It was half past eleven when they arrived at the club and the line for the Red Room was around the corner. Jake was pleased to see that the nightclub, which was almost two years old, was still a hot spot in Hollywood where the trends changed daily. Their driver pulled the black stretch Hummer to a stop in front of the club then came around to open the door. All of the ladies piled out followed by Jake, who was met with cheers from those waiting in line and camera flashes from the paparazzi.

Tamara and Nicole each hung from Jake's arms ensuring they'd be memorialized in print, while Amanda and Charlie hooked arms and walked in behind them; the blare of the music so loud it could be heard clearly on the street.

"Ladies and gentlemen in the house tonight, Red Room's owner, Mr. Jake Logan, and his four lovely ladies. Give it up for him, y'all!" the DJ announced, directing a spotlight toward the group as they climbed the steps to the VIP balcony.

Everyone applauded before the music started again, the bass pounding through the speakers in a steady pulse triggering the collective movement of a multitude of arms and legs.

The club boasted six spacious VIP balconies that overlooked the main dance floor, each having access to the private bar and equipped with plush red velvet couches and a personal waiter. The four-foot high parapets were padded; creating cushioned enclosures that prevented anyone from falling and getting hurt or from toppling over the side in a drunken stupor.

"If anyone needs anything just tell Kandi," Jake yelled over the music, pointing to a smiling waitress.

Nicole immediately began moving to the music. "Let's dance," she said to Jake, pulling his hand and shaking her hips against him.

Charlie leaned against the padded rail and scanned the crowd hoping she'd see Char, but the undulating sea of people prevented any immediate recognition. She decided that no matter what she'd check the restroom at midnight. She turned around to see Jake dancing with all three ladies; hands in the air as the girls moved around him in one rhythmic orgy. Leaving the scene behind her she went to the waitress and asked for a Mai Tai and had her drink in hand a few minutes later.

After a few songs passed Amanda moved from the group and came over to Charlie. "You okay, Char? Don't tell me doctors don't dance," she yelled so she could be heard over the sound of another fast song.

Charlie threw her head back and laughed, the drink giving her a nice buzz. "We dance, its just some things require liquid courage." She took another long sip of her drink, noting it was much stronger than any she'd made at the house, and stood up. She moved in place for a while, closing her eyes and snapping her fingers, feeling the beat of the song. Amanda went in search of Kandi to get a drink of her own and Charlie went back to the railing to search the crowd again for any sign of Char. She was still dancing when she felt Jake's huge hands encircle her waist as he moved behind her.

"This dress should be illegal for what it's doin' to me right now."

Charlie shivered as his warm breath caressed her ear, pushing back into him as their hips moved in rhythm to the music. He had her pinned by the railing and took full advantage of that fact, grinding his pelvis into her soft round bottom. She could feel his dick through his jeans and she teased the spot, making him press harder against her while his hands trailed over the bit of exposed skin between her minidress and the thigh-high boots. She leaned her head against his chest and placed her free hand on his muscular thigh, thoroughly turned on as she continued to move in time with his seductive cadence. Minutes later she picked a familiar face out of the crowd and their eyes locked.

It was time to go.

Still dancing, she turned to face Jake, getting one last long look. Hot tears pressed behind her eyes but she forced them back, concentrating on the man before her who was staring at her with the same intensity she'd seen a couple nights before on the roof. Setting her drink on the rail she wrapped her arms around his neck and he brought his hands to her rear, pulling her closer. Nestled in the curve of his hips she could feel his erection growing, and before she could give herself time to think she crushed her lips to his, kissing him hungrily for the last time. Her tongue slid into his hot mouth, and she teased, licked, and tasted every inch of it, moaning with a mix of pleasure and regret.

Tamara began dancing behind Jake, trying to interrupt their passionate moment, but both he and Charlie were too far gone. The song switched and Charlie reluctantly pulled away, catching her breath, tempted to kiss him again as he slowly licked his lips and his eyes opened.

She wiped her smeared lip gloss from his mouth with her thumbs then hugged him close and whispered in his ear, "Be right back." She pressed one last kiss to his neck and walked away.

Jake stayed at the rail with a satisfied smile on his lips, watching and enjoying how her hips and ass swayed while she walked to the stairs, and turning so he could follow her as she moved through the crowded dance floor below.

"You seem pretty serious about her, Tank," Tamara said, standing close beside him so he could hear her and staring out at the crowd with him. "Don't tell me you're in love with her already?"

"Why should you care, Tamara? You're only here for the drama factor and you know it."

Tamara shook her head, looking at him sadly. "You're wrong, Jake. I'm here for you, and I want you to give us another chance. I really miss you, Tank. You wanna wait 'til everyone leaves at closing and I'll show you?" she asked, snaking her hand around his waist.

He frowned down at her and pushed her arm away. "So we're supposed to pick up right where we left off, huh? You're in love with me now? 'Cause you sure as hell weren't the first three years."

"I made a mistake leaving you. But I always cared for you, Jake. I just didn't know how to show it. I'm here because I have your best interests at heart." She glanced back at the people dancing below, the wicked grin returning to her face. "Which may be more than I can say for Charlene at the moment."

Jake's view went back to the dance floor just as a man leaned close to Charlie to say something in her ear. Then she nodded and he grabbed her arm, pulling her through the crowd and toward the restrooms.

An overwhelming sense of possessiveness and jealousy struck, and Jake forced himself to unclench his fists. Remaining calm was essential, especially in front of Tamara who would definitely use this to her advantage.

"Maybe you're just seeing what you want to see in her, Tank," Tamara smirked.

Heart thudding in his chest, Jake turned and went down the stairs. He pushed his way recklessly through the crowd, anger rising to full boil. No way would he let another guy get close to his woman.

And dammit, Char was his.

* * * *

I was being pulled through the crowd by the one person in life I despise the most; who also happened to be the only person on earth Char and I could trust to help with the switch.

Tyler released my arm as we entered a hallway that led to the ladies room. The loud music was slightly dampened here, but not by much.

"She's inside," he said gruffly when we reached our destination. "Maybe *you* can talk some sense into her."

I had no idea what that meant so I didn't try to figure it out. I pushed through the heavy doors and entered a place of near serenity compared to the cacophonous sound of the club, expecting to be dab-smack in the center of a packed, filthy little bathroom. Imagine my surprise to find the place was spotless, and I silently applauded Jake's staff. Two women were checking their makeup in a large mirror and another jean-clad figure leaned against the far wall. Aside from that the space was deserted, which confused me thoroughly since I was searching for a woman wearing a magenta mini dress and my face.

"Charlie," Char called, waving me over to her.

"What the hell? Why didn't you wear the dress? And your hair isn't curled." I stated, hugging her tightly. For as much as I blamed her for the mess I was in, I'd really missed her.

The two women glanced at us, did a last minute check in the mirror, then left the room to return to the dance floor.

"Come on," I urged. "We gotta change."

"Charlie, stop," Char said calmly, shaking her head. "We can't switch."

"We *have* to switch, and fast, might I add. I don't know when I'll win another challenge or when we'll have another date. Tonight's perfect," I said rapidly, pulling at the zipper of one thigh-high boot. "Oh, his ex, Tamara, she's here, too. The other girls are—"

"Sweets, stop," Char interrupted firmly, grasping my shoulders and giving me a little shake. "We're not switching."

"We're… why not? That was the plan. I know it took a little while, but you can still get—"

"You don't hear well, do you? We're not switching because I know how you feel about him. I know you're fallin' for him, sweets."

I opened my mouth to protest then snapped it shut.

"Call it twin intuition," she smirked. "Look, it was a bad idea in the first place. But it would be even worse if I went out there pretending to have feelings for him when you really do. I saw you two dancing up there, all slow and seductive. And from that kiss he just gave you, I'd say he's diggin' you, too. I can't stand in the way of that."

So that's what Tyler meant.

"What about advancing your career?" I asked because I felt obligated, but a wave of excitement was already rising in my belly and I was doing a happy dance in my head.

Char waved the thought away with a flick of her wrist. "Tyler's an idiot. You and I both know these shows are only fifteen minutes of fame. I need a couple hours at least," she giggled. "Besides, if modeling doesn't work out I'll get into something else—maybe use that communications degree I earned for more than just a placeholder on our wall. Or singing. I like singing. By the way, you're rockin' that dress, sweets. You look great," she beamed.

"Thanks, Char. Wait," I frowned as a new thought struck me. "Did you know we weren't gonna switch *before* you decided on this particular ensemble?"

"Umm—"

"Remind me to kick you later," I deadpanned.

She laughed again. "I wanted to make sure Jake got a good view tonight. So get back out there and get your man, sweets."

"I love you," I said, embracing her again.

"Love you back!"

I walked out the bathroom feeling a thousand times better, met by the rising noise of the club—and an angry-looking Jake. I could tell he was straining for calm as his dark eyes narrowed slightly at the sight of me.

"Hey, Logan," I said surprised. "You okay? You look upset."

"Who's the guy you were with, Char?"

"Guy?" I asked perplexed, having completely forgotten about Tyler since I was so excited to be staying in the house and my mental happy dance must have been crushing brain cells.

"About this tall, slim build, white shirt, short hair…"Jake prompted, hands flying in description.

Char opened the bathroom door and froze, not expecting to run into me, and certainly not with Jake. He glanced up just as she dropped her head to her purse, searching through its depths for god-knows-what. She made a real show of it, taking a few steps while rummaging through the large bag until she was clear of us both. Then she strode down the hall quickly and dissolved into the crowd.

He stared at her retreating form for what seemed an eternity, a quizzical look on his face. I had no idea if he'd recognized her or not, so I decided to regain his attention with the truth. "Oh, him. He's a friend of my sister's. His name's Tyler."

He returned his gaze to my face, trying to determine if I was telling him the truth.

"Where'd he go? I told him to give me a minute," I asked, scanning the hallway although I knew Tyler's slimy ass was long gone.

"He took off when he saw me coming."

"Why Jake, I do believe you were jealous," I teased, grinning up at him. "Now you know half of what I've gone through these last few weeks living in that house, every girl fighting for your attention."

"Yeah, well, it's a damn uncomfortable situation," he admitted.

I placed my palms on his chest and felt some of the tension ebb from him. "I'm flattered that you were concerned, but I swear to you, Logan, he's a friend of my sister's. No other man holds a candle to you. No bullshit, and no pretense."

He leaned his back against the wall, pulling me into him by my waist so I was standing between his legs. "There're a lot of guys in this club, Char, and any of them would try to get with you. I just want to make sure you're not confused about who you're here for."

I nuzzled against him, sliding my hands down his chest and around has waist, finally feeling carefree after three weeks of lies. "Trust me, Logan. Coming to the club tonight just made it all the more clear."

Chapter 11
{*Day 26*}

Sundays are great! No competitions. No eliminations. And Jake can choose anyone he wants to go on an outing with. The only catch is that the girls choose the destination and activity.

The first Sunday, the wild bunch and Amanda took Jake to an amusement park. When they got back they had a ton of stuffed animals and souvenirs, and overall seemed like they had a fun time. The Sunday after that Tabitha and friends took Jake shopping. When they returned with their shopping bags stocked with shoes, clothes, and accessories, Jake—who was empty-handed—looked thankful the day was over.

Today he'd chosen me for a solo date! And I knew exactly where I'd take him.

I was coming out of the bathroom after applying a light dusting of makeup when Tamara stopped by my room.

"It's obvious Jake's quite taken by you, Charlene," she said matter-of-factly in that prim and proper way of hers. "I recognized it as soon as I came into the house yesterday."

I remained silent, not really knowing—or caring—where this conversation was going. I continued about the room, packing my bag with sunscreen, a few items of makeup, a swimsuit, sunglasses,and other random things.

"You might have fooled him, but you won't fool me. I know that guy the other night was more than just a friend."

"Tamara, you couldn't be more wrong. Truth is I can't stand the guy, but he knows my sister and I wasn't just gonna ignore him." I zipped and buttoned the teensy khaki shorts I was wearing; noting how they made my butt look great and my long, shapely legs look even longer and shapelier. Which probably explains why Char loves 'em. I vowed to venture into Char's crazy closet more often.

Tamara stood leaning against the doorjamb, arms folded under implants that were threatening to breach the tube top she was wearing.

"Whatever, Charlene. Just understand this. Jake and I already have a connection. He thinks he feels something for you only because I haven't been here. But things are definitely about to change. I'm not just his ex-girlfriend. I'm his ex-*fiancée*. He was glad to find out I was staying—in fact, he suggested it—and he asked me if we were gonna pick up where we left off."

I put on a lavender wrap-around blouse, securing the tie in the front, and put on some earrings as she continued her psychotic monologue.

"So whatever little tricks you think you have up your sleeve, you're already steps behind me. We were together for three years, Charlene. *Three years!* You don't just forget someone after that long. I still remember every kiss, caress, and smile."

I slid on my sandals and grabbed my bag and still she droned on.

"We've been through way too much to just let that go. A love like ours is rare, Charlene. I *will* get Jake back, and I—"

"Holy hell! Are you still talking?"

Tamara snapped her mouth shut, eyes bulging in disbelief, apparently unaccustomed to people challenging her domineering personality.

I continued the tirade that had been building since her arrival and subsequent needling the day she entered the house, getting in her face so I could stare her in her trifling eyes. "Listen, unless you've got something new and exciting to tell me, like how to milk a duck, shut the hell up! However it turns out, whether Jake chooses me or not, I'd bet money he's not choosing you, Tamara, if only on the premise that your asinine rambling will drive him crazy. In fact, I'm positive that had a good deal to do with why *he* dumped *you* in the first place! I swear, given the time and opportunity I'd have you committed to the nearest sanitarium *a priori*, because *clearly* you're certifiable, but as it happens I've got a date."

I pushed past the dumbfounded woman and swept down the two flights of stairs and out the door. The sun was shining brightly, I was feeling great in spite of the confrontation with Tamara, and the most delicious-looking man on the planet was waiting for me with a huge smile on his face.

"Hey, Logan."

"Hey, angel-face," Jake said pecking my lips once I reached the stretch Hummer. He wore soft blue jeans with a short-sleeved striped blue and white shirt, and a pair of white sneakers and looked great as always. I turned back to the house to find Tamara glaring at me from the doorway, suppressing the urge to say something. Jake glanced at her and back at me, picking up on the silent war we were fighting. "What's that all about?" he asked in his low timbre.

I looked in her direction and shrugged. "Maybe she figured out how to milk a duck already," I said thoughtfully. He looked at me puzzled and I waved the comment away and cringed, "Is she really staying, Logan?"

He rolled his eyes and sighed. "Yeah. Not much I can do about it except ignore her. You okay with that?"

"She's not an issue."

"Great," he said, his smile returning. "What's in store for today?"

"It's a surprise!" I beamed at him before climbing in.

The interior of the truck was amazing, with a plush leather bench lining one side of the vehicle and a fully stocked glass bar lining the other. The rear bench had been removed to accommodate a large flat screen television, and the ceiling was lined with recessed indirect lights and mirrors. I moved to the end of the bench closest to the privacy screen and once Jake was seated beside me, I slipped a blindfold over his eyes.

"This should be interesting," he said, rubbing my thigh as we pulled onto the main street. "Can I guess where we're going?"

"Sure! Three tries. But I bet you won't get it."

"I'll take that bet," he said as he swiveled to stretch out onto his back, laying his head in my lap and one hand on his chest. "And what do I get if I win?" he asked, making himself comfortable and adjusting the blindfold.

"The answer," I giggled, lightly slapping his hands from his face. "No peeking."

"I was hoping for a little more incentive, Char."

I threaded my fingers through the hand that rested on his chest. "I'll surprise you. Now guess already. We'll be there soon."

"A clue! Okay, so it's close and by my incredible sense of direction it feels like we're going east,"—he paused—"Is the zoo to the east?"

"Is that your first guess?"

"Yeah. You're taking me to the zoo."

"Steee-rike one! The zoo's not my idea of a great solo date, and for the record we're going west. Incredible sense of direction..." I mumbled, trailing off.

Jake laughed. "Busted. I actually use the GPS in my car. All right, we're going west. Another clue. The mall? Wait, no, you hate shopping."

"Nope, that counts," I said hurriedly. "Swing and a miss! Two strikes, baby."

He thought hard for a moment and then said assuredly, "I got it! You love to ride and there's a Harley shop this way. You're getting me on a bike!"

"Umm... Did you see what I'm wearing? I have on sandals, Logan. I never ride in sandals because toes come in handy every now and then."

"Yeah, I saw what you're wearing, but I stopped at those sexy little shorts. My eyes didn't make it down to your footwear," he brought my hand up to brush my knuckles with his lips.

"Three strikes and you're out. Sorry, babe. You'll just have to wait another minute," I said cheerfully.

"What were you gonna give me if I guessed right?"

I leaned over and kissed him deeply well after we'd arrived at our destination; loving the sweet taste of him; loving the way he felt in my mouth; loving the way he ran his hand through my hair as our tongues mingled and danced in their embrace. It felt absolutely perfect.

"Mmmm," he hummed when we parted. "Guess I'll have to try harder next time. Anymore where that came from?"

"Plenty," I replied, pecking his unsuspecting lips again. "But we're here."

"Is 'here' gonna be worth it, or could we just stay in the car?"

I thought about it, truly tempted. Kissing Logan was like heaven, but I really wanted to share this surprise with him. Plus, I had some confessing to do that definitely wouldn't happen if we stayed in the car.

"It's worth it," I said, reluctantly helping him from my lap. "You can take that blindfold off now."

As we emerged from the truck Jake took in his surroundings with a blank expression. "I've been to the

Santa Monica Pier before, Char. In comparison to the Hummer, it's not worth it," he smirked.

"O, ye of little faith." I grabbed his hand, pulling him down the beach away from the main pier. "C'mon."

As we approached the docks Jake's blank expression had become an ear-to-ear grin like a kid at Christmas. Even his eyes were smiling!

"You didn't?" he asked, now practically dragging me down the harbor as his stride lengthened.

"Uh-huh," I smiled back. "The white one on the end."

"Only you would think of something like this! Thank you, angel-face." He squeezed me close as we reached the fifty-foot sailboat and climbed aboard.

"I just hope you can handle this thing, because it's you, me, and the camera crew for the day."

He stood on the deck and looked around, not with concern at my statement, but with near disbelief that he was back on a boat. He looked genuinely happy and it warmed my heart that I could do it for him.

"I think we can manage," he answered as if remembering I'd said something. "Is there any food?"

"Yep. Hungry?"

He shook his head. "Not yet. We can eat once we get out a ways. But could you bring up something to drink? I'll get everything started up here."

"Aye aye, Cap'n." I saluted formally and went below deck.

Yesterday when I found out I'd gotten the Sunday date—and that it was a solo—the idea came to me instantly, and it was a mad rush to get this boat. I put in a call to Char who called a friend who said I could borrow his for the day. I didn't think to ask Char any details other than where it was docked, so I was pleasantly surprised when we arrived to see the beautiful vessel, ironically named *Charlemagne's Pursuit*. I threw my bag on the galley counter and strolled around, admiring first the salon, which was bright and beautifully appointed with a multitude of deck hatches and ports so you could get a clear view of the ocean from the inside. It was also very spacious which, considering Jake's height, was a major plus. The sofas were covered in butter-soft vanilla leather that accentuated the lacquered teak wood. To top it off, the aft stateroom had a roomy king-sized bed. I secretly hoped it would come in handy.

Char had come in early this morning and stocked the galley with bottled water, sodas, champagne, sliced fruit, sandwiches, and all the ingredients I needed to make my famous crab cannellonies and a salad. She even managed to get me two chocolate tarts from Spun Sugar, my favorite bakery. Everything was perfect.

I grabbed the champagne from the fridge and two glasses, and went back up the narrow steps. By the time I reached the deck, Jake was already guiding the boat out of the berth.

"Guess you know what you're doing, then. Let me know if you need any help," I offered, settling the flutes in the cup holders and filling them before taking a seat in the second lush captain's chair. As I looked around I noticed we were already a good ways from shore, but I could just make out three black-clad figures holding a variety of equipment. I shook my head, chuckling at what he'd done. "Aren't we short a few folks, Logan?"

Jake's brows were knit in concentration as he maneuvered around boats on our way out to sea. "I like the idea of it just being me and you today, so I told 'em to leave. You don't mind, do you?" he asked, throwing me a silky grin.

"Are you kidding? I'm finally getting some real alone time with you. No cameras. No other girls. Just you, me, and the ocean. Will the producers be mad?"

His face turned stormy in a flash and I instantly regretted asking. "After that stunt they pulled bringing Tamara here, I should sail right over to Hawaii and not come back. She wasn't part of the deal and they know it."

He was quiet a minute, silently fuming.

"Hey," I said softly, standing behind him and curling my arms around his chest. "You, me, and the ocean, right?" I gently pressed a kiss to his shoulder.

Jake nodded, but I could still feel the tension in him and I wasn't sure how to take that. Was he upset by her presence or did he still have some residual feelings for his ex-fiancée? A feeling of uncertainty washed over me, but I pushed it aside and tried to lighten the mood. "So, when do I get to drive this thing?"

That got a hearty laugh. "When we get a little further out I'll let you cut lose angel-face. I'd hate for you to have an accident and wreck something so beautiful... or this boat," he said. "You have your boating license?"

"Nope. I haven't been on a boat since I was a kid. I'm a land-lover, Logan. Open road and all that," I said, waving my hand in the air. "This was all about you. I wanted to see you at your happiest and so far I like it a lot."

"You've never had a shoot on a boat?"

"Nope," I answered quickly because it was too early to confess. "And where are you taking me? I'm not exactly prepared for Hawaii, but I won't complain."

"I thought maybe we'd go out to the Channel Islands Park. It doesn't take long to get there. You need reservations to dock, so we'll have to stop short of the island itself, but the view is still great from the boat. We can visit the park next time."

I grinned, watching as he maneuvered the sails, noting that he was already making future plans that included me and doing my happy dance in my head. And then I remembered that if I didn't say what I needed to soon, there'd be no next time. On the other hand, if I said what I needed to there might not be a next time either. Talk about a paradox. I decided to wait until we stopped.

True to his word, after we were about ten miles out to sea and no other boats were around, he had me stand in front of him, both our hands on the wheel as he showed me how to guide the boat; how the feel of the ocean, like the feel of the road, had to be respected or you'd go off course. He took his hands off the wheel and wrapped them about my waist, pointing out different aspects of the boat, the control panel, how the blue and white sails were worked. His deep voice caressed my ear as he held me close, and that he trusted me enough to let go meant a lot to me. We stayed like that for a long time and he rested his head against mine, enjoying the ride. As we neared our destination he took over again, teaching me how to slow the boat by turning it into the wind, and dropping anchor once we'd stopped.

So there we were, bobbing slightly in the vast expanse of the cobalt blue Pacific, just the two of us, a couple miles away from the reef that surrounded the island park. In the slightly cloudy water below I could make out colorful schools of fish and aquatic fauna, and the lush green island beyond looked inviting. I smiled again thinking about the next time I'd come here with Jake and watching him move about the boat checking lines.

"You want a snack, then maybe a swim before dinner?" I asked when he was done.

"You're cooking?"

I punched his arm and cut my eyes at him while he rubbed the spot. "I told you I'm a good cook."

"And I believe you, angel-face, although it's under duress," he teased.

"So what's it gonna be, Logan?" I turned to open the cabin door that led down the narrow salon steps.

"Say it again."

"What's it—"

"The last part."

I pivoted, caught by the seductive look in his brown eyes, fully understanding what he implied. "Logan," I said a little breathless.

His lids lowered to half-mast and his face slid into its easy grin. "Come here, Char."

I took a small step forward when hearing my twin's name echo in my head made my brain over-rule my limbs, fighting traitorous legs that were trying to move me toward him. My body was responding to his look alone, nipples hardening, belly fluttering, pulse racing. It would be so easy to just fall into his arms and forget about my little lie, but I had to come clean first. It was now or never; and never was looking really good right now.

"Jake, I—I need to talk to you about something," I said nervously.

He frowned. "Well *that* sounds ominous. Can this 'something' be bad news in any way? You have a boyfriend? You married? Got kids?"

I shook my head vigorously. "No. Very much available… and without offspring."

"You have warrants or a felony I should know about?"

I chuckled at his attempt at levity. "No, but you still might think it's bad news."

He turned his gaze back to the ocean, the sun reflecting brightly off the blue water making him squint, but he stared at it nonetheless. He slowly closed the short distance between us and placed his hands on my shoulders, kneading them gently as he looked into my eyes.

"Whatever it is, tell me later. Today's been the best day I've had in a long time, and I don't want anything to ruin it, okay?"

Against my better judgment I looked into his sexy brown eyes and agreed. Despite the fact that I desperately needed to get this off my chest before things went further, that's exactly where they went.

"C'mon," he whispered, guiding me to the cabin doors and down into the salon. He grasped my hand and looked about quickly, admiring the elaborate space before gently nudging me toward the aft bedroom, his chest pressed to my back, his arms encircled about my waist as he dropped those sweet kisses on my neck.

As we entered I saw a note on the wine-colored comforter. Noticing Char's elegant handwriting, I picked it up and read it, Jake reading over my shoulder.

Sweets,

> *Call it a hunch that you'd make it in here.*
> *Check the drawer. Don't behave!*
> *Love you,*
>> *Lil Sis* ☺

He moved to the small dresser in the room and opened the top drawer, a huge smile on his face as he reached in for the surprise Char had tucked inside. "Twelve pack. I like your little sister already."

* * * *

Jake tossed the box of condoms on the bed and brought Charlie back into his arms. "We don't have to do anything you don't want to," he said, bending to touch his forehead to hers as he massaged her lower back with his fingers.

She slid her arms around his neck in response and kissed him, his tongue sliding past her soft lips and into her hot mouth, caressing her tongue in a sensual rhythm. She drew his bottom lip into her mouth, sucking gently, eliciting a soft moan from Jake who angled her head back to deepen the kiss. She backed him to the wall, unbuttoning his shirt and running her fingertips over his bare skin. She eased the shirt off his broad shoulders and let it drop to the floor, kissing his chin and down his neck before dropping her lips to his collarbone, brushing the area softly. His warm hands palmed the globes of her bottom through the shorts, squeezing playfully as he pressed her against his bulging erection.

She smoothed her hand across his chest, feeling his strong heartbeat thudding beneath her palm as she lightly nibbled a hard male nipple, inhaling his intoxicating masculine scent. Then she let it trail down his torso, tracing each of his well-defined abs with a feather-light caress, lower, lower until she reached his belt.

An electric current rushed straight to Jake's groin with her every movement, her soft touch against his hard body nearly driving him insane. The anticipation of her next move was wild excitement and maddening torture at the same time. He'd waited nearly two months for this moment and was determined to take his time learning every inch of this woman—*his* woman—that is unless she kept up this sweet agony, in which case he'd have to take her hard and fast and learn her later. Momentarily tempted by the thought, he grasped her hand, stopping her before she had him fully undressed. Watching her through lust-lidded eyes, his breathing harsh and ragged, he said, "Strip for me, angel-face."

Charlie grinned seductively at the challenge, toeing off her sandals. Keeping her eyes on Jake she reached for the tie in her shirt and tugged, causing the scant bit of fabric to separate revealing an Italian-style white lace bra. Flipping her dark curly hair off her shoulders, she slowly removed the shirt, hearing his breath catch with the sight of her hardened nipples pressing through the nearly sheer lingerie. She stood before him, her hands playing at the band of her shorts before she unfastened the hasp and gripped the two sides pulling them apart, the zipper sighing as it made it's two-inch trek from top to bottom. She folded the sides down to reveal a hint of matching white lace panties. She paused, watching Jake watch her, the tip of his tongue caught between his top teeth and bottom lip, waiting for her to slide the shorts over her hips, his eyes glazed with desire. She inched them down further, more lace exposed, then turned away from him and bent slightly at the waist—just a teeny bit—rolling her hips slowly as she pushed the tight khakis over her rounded bottom and the rest of the way down her hips, letting them fall down her shapely legs and pool at her feet.

With a flirty glance over her shoulder she saw Jake lick his lips, his eyes glued to cheeks hanging slightly from the lacy panties. Stepping out of the shorts she sauntered the five feet to the bed and spun to sit on the comforter facing him. "Your turn, Logan."

Jake moved to stand before her, stepping out of his shoes on the way. Charlie grasped his waistband and kissed around his navel, licking and kissing his abs as he pushed her back on the bed, lying between her splayed legs. He tugged down the thin material of her bra, letting her full breasts spill over the band. He palmed one with a hand, tugging gently at the distended nipple. He laved hungrily at the other breast before drawing that nipple into his mouth and trapping it in his teeth, glancing the tip of his tongue over the sensitive flesh.

"Oh, god," she moaned. She brought her hand to the breast he had in his mouth, squeezing the flesh in offering as he opened wider to take it all in, sucking and biting, the pleasure-pain thrilling Charlie as she whimpered softly in the back of her throat. "That feels so good, Jake," she breathed as he switched to show the other orb the same attention.

Charlie was melting, a simmering liquid pool starting between her thighs and radiating throughout her body as Jake licked and fondled her breasts. She rubbed her hands over his naked back and shoulders, writhing beneath him as he trailed kisses down her belly then moved to lick up the length of her inner thigh, nipping and grazing the delicate skin. His big hands rubbed her legs as he buried his nose in her sex, inhaling the heady scent of her and pressing a solid kiss to the damp panties.

"You smell so sweet, baby," he murmured. "I knew you would." She shuddered as he pulled the panties down and off her legs, revealing the soft dark curls of her wet womanhood. He stepped back, eyes drinking in the sight of her pliant brown body against the crimson comforter. "I've been thinking about this for too damn long. You're so beautiful, angel-face," he said thickly, working the belt free and unfastening his pants. He pushed the jeans and boxers down, his hard erection springing free. His muscles rippled as he kicked his feet free of the clothing.

Charlie stared at the magnificent man standing nude before her, trying to commit every inch of his statuesque body to memory. She licked her lips at the sight of his long, thick cock, her heart thumping a skittered one-two in expectation as she watched him pull a condom from the box and rip it open swiftly. She sat up, one hand joining his as he rolled it on, until she alone fisted his shaft, a slow up and down motion over his rigid length as his head fell back, moaning beneath her touch. Her other hand came to his lightly furred thigh, gently caressing the muscled limb. A jolt raced through his body with each stroke, making his abs clench.

Jake bent to find her lips, kissing her fiercely as he laid her back and she spread her thighs so he could settle between them. With the thick head of his cock positioned at her slick entrance he teased and tortured her, glancing across her clit and down her slit over and over again, until he was swallowing her pleading whines and she was lifting her hips from the bed, begging him to enter her.

Charlie cried out as Jake sank into her slowly, stretching her, invading her, filling her inch by painstaking inch, until he was seated fully inside her. He didn't move for a moment letting her adjust to the size of him and loving the feel of her sheathed tightly about him. Slowly, he began stroking her, loving her passionately as if they'd always been lovers, her arms moving with familiarity across his back and over his head. He bent her leg toward her, supporting it and bracing it open with a strong forearm under her knee, making her moan as he drove deeper into her warmth. His lips found her neck, drawing the skin into his mouth and sucking. She grasped his shoulders, pressing him to her as she clenched and released her pelvic muscles, milking and massaging his hard length. The motion sent a new wave of arousal through him as he pumped his hips harder and growled, biting her neck firmly and marking her.

"Yes, Logan," she hissed, feeling her orgasm close. "That's it, baby."

"Damn, you feel so good." Jake moved faster, wrapping her other leg around him without missing a stroke, reaching a new depth. "You like that, yeah," he stated, sweat dripping down his sculpted chest.

"Mmm hmm," she mumbled low in her throat biting her lip, arching her back to take him deeper. Her arms went over her head, grabbing for purchase among the comforter, fisting the material in her hands.

"Tell me. Let me hear you, angel-face," he demanded roughly, shifting his angle.

"Oh, god! Yes!" She screamed with delight at the unexpected change, her heart pounding in her head. "Right there, Logan! Oh my...yeah, J! Yeah, yeah, yeah!"

Jake pulled back and lifted off her, slowing the rhythm just as she was about to go over the brink, torturing her with long deep thrusts. Her chest heaved, her lids fluttered open and she fixed him with a lusty gaze.

"You're... killin' me," she whimpered faintly between gasps, "know that?"

He grinned down at her and, continuing his stroke, he yanked her to the edge of the bed so his feet were set firmly on the ground. "Am I?" he asked, repeatedly plunging into her swiftly, the impact of their bodies meeting with a SMACK! before pulling nearly completely out of her again.

She nodded her head slightly, tugging at the comforter still gripped in her hands.

"Good," he said thickly, looking down at the spot where their bodies met, burning the image into his memory, watching as he buried himself balls deep inside her tight folds and withdrew again, willing himself not to lose control at the sight of her cream on his cock. "I want you to remember you're mine."

With that statement she tightened her legs around him as he brought his hands to her belly, letting them roam across her body while he sank back into her. He brought a hand between them, spreading her labia and finding her clit.

"I want you to remember I was here; want you to feel me every time you think about me, and know that you belong with me." He flicked the nub gently with his thumb, sending rounds of delicious shivers through her, then pressed harder as he increased the pace of his thrusts, the sound of skin slapping skin playing a harmonic melody.

"Oh god, Logan!" Charlie screamed, her voice wrenched from a place deep in her soul. "Please don't stop. Don't stop! Don't stop! Right there, Logan!"

He bent over her, continuing to stroke her pussy and tease her clit, the rush of liquid pooling around his shaft and finger.

"Now, baby," he whispered against her skin then nipped her. "Come for me right now, angel-face."

On cue Charlie's orgasm peaked, feeling her hot juices sliding down her ass while Jake continued to drive into her. Her tight channel fluttered and rippled around him with the force of her climax, and she whimpered as her legs and belly shook from the intensity, involuntarily arching her body off the bed and thrusting her breasts toward his waiting mouth. Jake suckled the mounds, wave after wave of pleasure passing through her while her vision blurred and muscles cramped.

Her chest rose and fell as she gulped down air, and as sanity returned she felt Jake still rock hard inside of her, a realization that turned her on all over again. She pressed his chest, and he rolled onto his back and moved them up the bed. He knew exactly what she wanted. From her new perch atop him, straddling him, Charlie bent her head to pepper his shoulder with kisses, her hair a dark wavy mass feathering his skin. He ran his hands up her thighs to her waist, sealing her to him as she sat up and rested her palms on his sweat-slicked chest. She rolled her hips against his, lifting slightly with each movement as Jake slammed her back into him. She felt him jerk with every action, and knew the divine friction was bringing him close to his own sweet nirvana.

They fell into a steady rhythm, Charlie moaning as she threw her head back, her hair cascading off her shoulders in a curly brown waterfall, breasts rising and falling in a sensual cadence. Jake reached up to caress them again, and Charlie bent to him, filling his hands with her soft rounded flesh, scraping her teeth down his jaw and feeling his heart race as she ground against him, riding him to ecstasy.

"Come on, baby," he urged, his voice straining as he brought his hands back to her ass, kneading and spreading the tissue while he pulled her back into him with every turn of her hips. His abs clenched, face turned into an ecstatic grimace.

She felt him grow impossibly harder, and he kissed her intensely, growling into her mouth when her nails bit into his shoulders with another climax, the feel of her juices pooling at the base of his shaft and down his tightly drawn balls triggering his own sublime release, shooting streams of hot fluid into the safety of the latex.

Charlie collapsed onto his heaving chest, shuddering and boneless and sated, breathing heavily as Jake continued to twitch and jerk inside her, pinning her to him with strong arms.

"Didn't hurt you, did I?" he rumbled when their breathing had steadied enough to formulate words.

She shook her head slightly making her wild hair dust his cheek. He smoothed it off her face and pressed a kiss to her sweaty temple.

Charlie's brain turned on in the afterglow, and all the confidence she felt before suddenly evaded her. As it stood, she and Jake weren't exactly a couple. Hell, she didn't even know if they'd be more than a one-boat-ride stand, regardless of whatever he'd said in the passion-induced moment. And though she'd never been in the position before, she was sure the post-coital niceties of a situation such as this—mind-blowing or not—did not include cuddling. After a moment she rolled off him and onto her back, the need to sleep hitting her like a sledgehammer.

Jake got up from the bed and went into the bathroom, the sound of running water a soothing melody to Charlie whose eyes fluttered closed. Minutes later she felt a warm wet towel being dabbed tenderly between her legs, cleaning her, followed by feather-light kisses on her belly. The bed shifted under his weight as he climbed back up and pulled the disheveled comforter and top sheet aside.

"Get under, baby," he whispered. Eyes still closed Charlie slid between the sheets, noticing they were warm in spots where they'd made love and cool in the few spots they'd missed. She rolled away a bit to be sure she wasn't crowding him.

"Come here, angel-face," he said as he settled his big body beside her. "I might be a bad boy, but I'm a cuddler." A soft giggle escaped her lips and Charlie rested her head on his chest, snuggling close and winding a leg around his. He wrapped his arm around her and pulled the covers over them. Her free hand came to rest over his heart, and he covered it with his own hand, pressing her warm palm to his chest.

"Are you hungry?" she mumbled, fighting sleep and losing.

"After that appetizer?" he chuckled.

Charlie yawned, too tired to comprehend the joke. "Just give me a few minutes, and I'll—"

"Shhh. Go to sleep, baby," he whispered, lazily stroking her hair and staring through the skylight at the bright day outside. Her breathing evened, a light stream of warm air escaping her parted lips and feathering across his chest.

Jake couldn't remember ever feeling so connected with a woman during sex—no, not just sex. That was definitely *more* than just sex. The truth had been hovering at the edge of his thoughts for a while, so the realization didn't come as a surprise. In fact, it settled on him like a blanket, warm and comforting, bringing a sense of long-desired balance and serenity.

Jake Logan had fallen—and he couldn't have been happier.

Charlie murmured softly in her sleep drawing his attention to her peaceful face. She looked even more angelic with her glowing eyes closed and her long dark lashes curved over her cheeks. The feel of her soft body pressed against him and the smell of their comingled juices heavy in the air caused a stirring low in his belly, and he considered bringing his hand to massage her silky flesh again before pushing the thought aside. Right now they had all the time in the world—no need to rush. He sighed contentedly and squeezed her gently, kissing the top of her head.

"Just you, me, and the ocean."

* * * *

I awoke to the gentle rocking of the boat, brilliant sunlight flooding through the aperture overhead, and a dull ache between my legs, but no Logan.

I got out of bed and noticed Jake's shirt was still in a heap against the wall. The rest of our clothes were littered across the floor, and I smiled at the proof that I hadn't been dreaming. Adjusting my bra—or more correctly, putting the girls back in it the way they should be—I tugged on my panties and slid on his shirt, swaddled in his scent as I fastened three middle buttons. It hung on me like a blue and white tent. Padding barefoot through the salon, I glanced at the clock—2:17 p.m.—and went up the skinny ladder to the deck. I looked around but didn't immediately see Jake, then caught a glimpse of his head toward the bow of the boat. I stretched out on the bench behind the captain's chairs and closed my eyes, letting the California sunshine warm my bare legs and face. For the first time in a long time I was really relaxed. I could definitely get used to this boating thing.

A few minutes later a shadow crossed my face and I smiled, opening my eyes to a bare-chested Logan, pants riding low on his hips accentuating his muscular abdominals.

"That looks good on you," Jake said, tugging at the material, "though it's a little big."

"Think so? Stole it from this *really* sexy guy I know. 'Bout your height… your build… goes by the name Logan. Ever met him?"

Jake chuckled. "Yeah, but I hear he's some bad-ass playboy type. A bonafide asshole. What's a pretty lady like you doing messin' with a good-for-nothin' guy like that?"

I rose up on my elbows. "Must be a different guy. The Logan I know is a real sweetheart. But don't tell him I told you, though. I'd hate to ruin his rep." I winked at him and giggled.

He settled on a captain's chair and spun to face me. "I didn't mean to wake you when I left."

"I'm a light sleeper. Comes with the job." He frowned and I remembered he had no idea what I really did for a living. I waved it off. "What got you up?"

"Honestly," he grinned, "I was really close to waking you up for round two."

- 154 -

My heart started pounding at the remembered feel of him over me, thrusting into me, kissing me. And just like that I was ready for him again. Too bad he had other ideas.

"Hungry, angel-face?" he asked, making a real effort at keeping his eyes on mine and not on my legs.

"Umm…yeah, sure," I stammered getting up, a gust of wind blowing the flaps of the shirt up revealing my white-laced ass. For some reason I was embarrassed, and it must have shown on my face.

Without missing a beat Jake said, "It's a really great ass, y'know. Nice and round and soft. You shouldn't cover it up." An easy smile was on his face as he stood up to stretch. "Plus I'm gonna see it again real soon anyway."

"Did you want sandwiches or the canellonies?" I asked, trying to keep from smiling. It's amazing how goofy sex makes you. Maybe cause the blood's going away from your brain.

"How long do we have the boat?"

"Ours for the day," I chirped, pecking his lips.

"Then let's stay all day." He dropped his hands to my waist and his forehead to mine. "So the sandwiches now. I'll come down and help—"

"No, you won't," I said, pushing him back into the chair and standing between his legs. "Today's about you, remember? So I'm playing stewardess to your captain."

His hands stroked slowly over my ass and came to rest at my thighs, tugging me a little closer. "And playmate to my playboy?" He stared up at me, cocking a sexy brow and licking his lower lip.

I nodded, sliding my hands onto his strong shoulders, the fluttering in my belly starting up all over again. "At least for today, Logan. Tonight it's back to the madhouse we go."

A serious looked crossed his face. "What if I want more than just today?"

Did I hear that right? My heart was pounding and my already mushy brain was turning—mushier. Was Jake Logan actually interested in me? Not just for the show? Ohmygod-ohmygod-ohmygod!

In spite of the fact that my happy dance was in full swing in my head and doing further damage to the few functioning brain cells I had left, I managed a casual tone. "Now Logan, what would a pretty lady like me be doing with a good-for-nothin' guy like you?"

"I can think of a few things," he said slyly, his hands going under the shirt and grasping the bands of my panties, pulling them down to my thighs. I kissed his lips as his warm hands smoothed down my belly and lower. Two strong fingers found my lower lips, separating them and his thumb pressed my sensitive nub.

I moaned into his mouth as those two thick digits entered me, stroking me slowly, and he used the heel of his hand to rub my clit causing tendrils of ecstasy to shoot through me like stars exploding. I rolled my hips trying to alleviate the mounting pressure, but that turned me on even more.

His other hand began working at the shirt, unbuttoning it and pushing it off me. He dropped his kisses lower; nibbling my stomach then licking my navel as he continued the most pleasurable assault on my most feminine parts I've ever had. With his free hand he deftly unhooked my bra and tossed it somewhere. He nudged me down and I ended up flat on my back on the no-slip deck, the coarse grainy surface rubbing against my skin.

Jake kissed my lips again, tugging the panties off fully to lie between my bent legs. Once they were gone I could feel his erection pressed against me through the stiff material of his jeans, the rough texture feeling delicious. He trailed his kisses lower, my body on fire, ready and aching. Before I knew it he had his shoulders under my knees, his hands grasping my thighs, licking them, moving closer.

He inhaled deeply then drew the tip of his tongue over my swollen lips, teasing the slit.

"Mmm, you taste good, angel-face. So tight and sweet," he said, before plunging his tongue deep inside of me, drinking in my juices.

It felt so good I got stuck between screaming and moaning, managing only a soft little whimper, my lower lip trapped between my teeth. My heart thudded against my ribcage and my hands caressed his head. This much pleasure had to be illegal somewhere; but not here, in the middle of the ocean on a boat with Logan. I thought it couldn't get any better when he put those two fingers inside me again, stroking fast, and his tongue feverishly brushed my clit, driving me absolutely bananas. The pressure mounted in my belly and I thought I'd burst with the climax that ripped through me.

I screamed, ears going fuzzy, but I could just make out the sound of a zipper unzipping, a rustling of clothing, and foil ripping.

With one rough thrust Jake was deep inside me again, arms planted on either side of me to support his weight. He drove into me with such force that we actually inched across the gravelly deck. I wrapped my arms around him and held on for the ride.

This was nothing like the first time. It was much more carnal, feral even, and I loved every bit of it. I got the impression he was doing more than having sex with me; he was learning me and how to please me. I lifted my hips to meet his thrusts, sending him into a tailspin and he started bucking harder, faster, deeper. His mouth was pressed to my ear and, damn, the steamy things he whispered...

I licked his neck just below his ear then bit him softly, trapping the sinewy cords between my teeth as I mewled with delight beneath him, making him growl deep in his throat.

I wrapped my legs around his hips and let him take control, plunging and thrusting and grinding until moments later we were both shuddering and shaking with bliss, sticky and tired and spent, gulping down the salty sea air. Tears streamed down my temples. Not from pain but from the onslaught of emotion and sensation and stimulation that I could sum up in one beautiful, sacred, extremely terrifying word.

We lay there holding onto each other, and I love the feel of Jake's weight on me. After a bit he rolled off me, still breathing heavily as we both stared up at the bright sky.

"You okay, angel-face? Too rough for you?"

I wriggled, trying to move my arm so I could wipe my eyes but I was too exhausted. "I'm fine, and that was amazing, but it's *definitely* gonna leave a bruise," I laughed, rolling onto my side to face him as his arm went around me, his other hand gently wiping the water from my temples. He looked at me with soft brown eyes and a faint smile on his lips like he knew exactly what I was feeling.

"You didn't answer me."

Answer him? I could barely think straight let alone string words together to form complex things like sentences. "'Bout what, Logan? Although it's really not fair for us to have brain-damaging sex then expect me to wax philosophic."

He chuckled, a low rumble in his chest that ran through me, rubbing his hand lazily along my back.

"You're right. It's not the right time." He kissed my forehead then angled his head against mine.

I let it go, but I knew exactly what he was talking about. If Jake Logan wanted more than just today, he could have it and then some. We lay there a while, side by side on the hard deck, staring up at the sunny blue sky as the boat rocked gently.

"Next Sunday you think we could go for a ride? I know you guys get to choose the activity for the date, but I think it'd be fun to be in your element, open road and all that."

Did he just choose me for next Sunday's date? My heart melted!

"You ever ride before?" I asked, trying to stay calm.

He scoffed in his deep timbre. "Doesn't every bad-ass playboy ride a bike, Char? It's mandatory or they kick you out of the club. Sweet little black Ducati GT 1000, though I don't ride it much. I don't think I've even taken it out of the city."

"What? You're kidding!" I exclaimed leaning up on my elbow to see his face. "My main bike's a red Ducati Streetfighter!"

"So you like to ride fast and hard, huh?"

"An affliction we both suffer, apparently."

The innuendo wasn't lost on him, and he grinned his sexy grin, making my stomach flip flop.

"The first night you said you ride whenever you need to think, but a Streetfighter's not really a cruiser. You have more than one bike?" he asked, somewhat surprised.

"Yeah, the Ducati, a Harley Road Glide, and a '62 Harley DuoGlide," I replied, thinking about mom's bike in the garage. "I'm rebuilding that one myself."

"I love a woman who gets her hands dirty," he stated in his rich voice, his brown eyes searching my face.

He let that hang in the air for what seemed an eternity. But in my current emotion-laden state, that comment floored me. Was that 'love' like 'I love chocolate'? Or was it something else? Or was it that I was *hoping* it was something else? *God, let it be something else!*

"So next Sunday we'll go riding then?"

I nodded excitedly, temporarily filing this latest entry to the growing list of things requiring analysis. "It's a date. Do I get my own bike?" I challenged.

"Would you have a problem riding behind me?"

"Ride pillion?" I asked using the proper term for what everyone else offensively called riding bitch. I knew he wasn't insulting me. Crazy as it sounds, if we were in a biker gang, riding pillion would mean I was his girl. "I think I could manage that."

He squeezed me a little tighter and a bizarre thought crossed my mind making me smile and Jake frown.

"What?"

"I was just thinking, I've never made love on a bike before, but the idea does have promise."

Jake pulled me on top of him, his erection pressing into my stomach. "Oh, I'm sure we'll figure out something, angel-face," he assured, kissing me lightly on the lips. "'Til then, we rock the boat."

Chapter 12
{*Day 27*}

I was still on cloud nine from yesterday, if a little sore in a "Jeez, I'm sore but I can't wait to do that again" kind of way because, frankly, it had been an abysmally long time. Four years to be exact. But it had never, and I mean *never*, been like that. It was passionate, and intense, and tender, and rough, and loving, and giving, and taking, and explosive, and absolutely the best sex I've ever had! Ever.

I'm pretty sure I have deck-burn somewhere on my low back and ass that perfectly compliment the passion marks on my neck, but damn it was all worth it. Jake definitely lived up to the Tank moniker his ex had given him. We spent the day talking and making love—in a variety of positions—and when we pulled back into the dock around seven, we spent another two hours below decks. We managed to christen ever nook and cranny on that boat, even a really narrow closet, fulfilling that vertical fantasy I'd had on day one. Even though I didn't get to cook, the chocolate tarts got eaten, but the method was slightly unorthodox. The man tasted great covered in chocolate. Something about Logan turned me into an absolute minx and I loved it. The only thing to slightly dampen my spirits was the fact that I didn't get to talk to him about the switcheroo Char and I had pulled.

"It's gotta be today," I resolved, pulling on a pair of dark denim walking shorts, a cap-sleeve high-collared yellow blouse to hide what the makeup couldn't of the plum colored bruises on my neck, and a pair of multi-colored heels. It was ten in the morning and I was finishing my hair and makeup when everyone was called to the living room.

As I entered I noticed only a few of the ladies had made it down already. I looked at Jake, who was even sexier today, wishing I could have woken up next to him this morning. Even though I'd showered on the boat, and again this morning, I could still smell him on my skin, still feel him inside my body, and taste him on my tongue. And seeing him in his jeans, a thin gray V-neck sweater with a white crew neck shirt beneath, and a pair of white sneakers, my body started reacting again, the way seeing chocolate makes your mouth water. I swallowed hard as his gaze went from my face, down my body and back up to my neck. He studied my blouse then gave me a knowing grin and a wink, before turning his attention back to the remaining ladies who entered.

"Okay," Jake began. "My family is really important to me, so over the next couple of days you're gonna meet a few people that are pivotal in my life. You'll spend a little time with each of them and they'll let me know what they think of you. I know it can be nerve-wracking, but just be yourselves, 'cause my people can spot a fake a mile away," he paused, staring directly at Tamara. He clapped his hands together as an older couple entered the room, "So first I'd like to introduce you to my parents, Anthony and Nathalie Logan."

We all clapped and cheered, and I noticed some of the more scantily clad girls made an attempt to pull their clothes together a bit.

Nathalie Logan was a beautiful woman with a pleasant smile, standing about five foot ten with a petite frame, long brown hair, honey-colored skin, and Jake's dark eyes. Her husband stood just to the side of her. He looked like an older version of Jake, though not nearly as tall standing some five inches shorter than his son with just a hint of gray in his short black hair. His arm was clasped around his wife's shoulder, hers about his waist, an easy smile on his face. Their connection was evident, almost tangible, and I watched as Jake smiled in admiration at the sight of his parents standing before us so obviously in love with each other.

"Hello, everyone," Nathalie smiled, scanning the crowd. "Aren't you all just beautiful? We're so happy to be able to get a chance to meet with you and learn a little about you."

"And to find out which one of you is right for our son," his father boomed in his deep baritone. Now I know where Jake got it.

"We're all going into the dining room for a little brunch first, and then my parents will spend some time with you in smaller groups, okay? Good. To the dining room."

Like lambs we trailed behind the Logan family, Jake at the fore, his parents cuddled together just behind like love-struck teenagers. It was the cutest thing I'd ever seen. We'd all be so lucky to experience just a tenth of the love they shared.

When we entered the dining room, Anthony gallantly pulled out a chair for his wife, and once she was seated, took his place at the end of the table. Jake sat opposite his father at the other end, the two Logan men in the positions of power. But after all the ladies had been seated—me across from his mother and nearest his father—and short introductions had been made, it quickly became apparent who was the real head honcho.

"So, down to brass tacks," Nathalie began as the catered meal was being served, "which one of you is right for my son and why?" She glanced at Tamara who was sitting by Jake, then at her son with a questioning frown. I saw Jake shrug and roll his eyes and I tried to suppress my giggle but made a noise like I was choking instead. I reached for my glass of water and took a sip.

"You okay, Charlene?" Anthony asked.

I nodded. "Yes, I'm fine, thank you."

Nathalie's eyes were on mine in an instant, openly appraising me. She shot another look at Jake slightly raising her brows. He looked to me, our eyes meeting briefly, then back to his mother. His lips curved into a grin as a plate was set before him. He thanked the server then turned his attention to the arduous task of settling his napkin across his lap. She returned her gaze to me, studying me like Jake had when we first met, and smiled broadly. I smiled back, feeling as if I'd just taken some unknown test and passed with flying colors.

* * * *

"So, how'd you two meet?" Charlie asked as everyone dined and the multiple conversations became a low din around her.

Nathalie glanced at her husband and smiled. "Actually, our parents introduced us."

Anthony beamed at Charlie, "And she hated my guts," he confided with a chuckle. "Couldn't stand me. In fact, when our parents *conspicuously* left the room, Nat here offered me a drink... of arsenic."

"Well, he was a perfectly pompous ass," Nathalie added matter-of-factly. "He figured because he was young, successful, and *mildly* attractive—"

"If by 'mildly' you mean insanely, then I agree with you whole-heartedly, dear... " he interrupted with mock sincerity.

Nathalie waved his comment away and continued "-that I'd instantly fall head-over-heels in love with him at first sight. Maybe his ex-girlfriends tripped when they saw him coming, but I had to make sure he knew I wasn't gonna be a push-over."

Anthony barked a laugh that Charlie decided sounded very much like his progeny's. "Yeah, she proved her point all right. We dated six months before she even let me kiss her!"

Charlie smiled back and forth between the two. "Aww. But she was worth the wait, right?" she commented.

Anthony leaned toward Charlie and said in a stage whisper, "Jury's still deliberating."

Nathalie arched a perfect brow. "Thirty-six years later? They'd have tossed the case out by now, honey."

"Oh, yeah?" Anthony asked sighing heavily and shrugging. "Then I guess I'm stuck with her now."

Charlie giggled as Nathalie slapped her husband's arm then deadpanned, "Like Velcro, sweetheart, so get used to it."

"Wouldn't have it any other way."

Charlie smiled at the couple's bantering, wondering if this could ever be her and Jake; madly in love and happy together. "So how did you know that this was the person you'd spend the rest of your life with?" she asked, pulling herself from her daydreaming and taking another drink of water.

"Apparently the statute of limitations has expired, so…" Anthony trailed off, laughing again when his wife shot him a 'keep it up' look. He chuckled and held up his hands palms out, "In all seriousness, I just knew. Nathalie knew who she was, what she wanted, and I admired that about her. She never tried to conform or be anyone she wasn't; strong and confident without being overbearing. And once I cracked that tough shell with my devastating charm and rugged good looks, I knew she was the only woman I'd ever want to be with for the rest of my life." He snapped out of his loving narrative long enough to make another joke. "Completely *ruining* me for any other woman."

Nathalie shook her head. "Incorrigible."

"Yeah, well your son is equally afflicted," Charlie assured, not realizing Jake had come up behind her, gripping the back of her chair.

"These two boring you, Char?" he asked.

"Not in the least, Logan," she said, angling her head up to see him and adding genuinely, "Your parents are great! Now I know where you get it from."

He smiled down at her lovingly, making her breath catch, before turning his attention back to his parent. "Well, I think we need to do the group meetings now if you're done eating. It'll be outside on the patio. I'll send the first group out."

They both nodded, standing from the table and twining fingers as they left the dining room.

Jake watched them go then rested his other palm on the table as he crouched near Charlie's ear so she could hear his low whisper. "I'm impressed. You seem to have worked your magic on my parents, too. My father's always been easy-going, but my mother usually takes a while to warm up to anyone I bring home."

She turned slightly to fix him with a steady gray-eyed gaze. "I meant it, Jake. Your parents really are great. You're lucky to have them."

"Lucky to have you, too, angel-face," he said then dropped his voice even lower, just a deep, breathy whisper against her ear. "I was up thinkin' about you all night. How sweet you taste. How good it felt to be inside you…feeling you come down my dick. You think about me?"

Charlie felt the heat rising and reached for her glass of water, taking a long swallow.

"I'll take that as a yes." He withdrew from her side and went about gathering the girls into groups to meet with his parents, leaving Charlie smiling at her vivid thoughts of yesterday and aching for a repeat performance.

* * * *

After a delicious brunch and a general interrogation, we broke into groups to be interrogated further by Jake's parents. I thought it was interesting that at the age of thirty-three, they were still protective of him like he was their little boy. A few of the girls in my group stuttered and stumbled when asked about their intentions with Jake; were they only after his money, how did they feel about kids, could they handle being with someone who was as social as Jake was. Of course everyone gave the "right" answer, but as I watched the three Logans go upstairs to Jake's room to talk, I felt confident that they could sort out the truth.

About twenty minutes later, the three descended the stairs looking as if they hadn't discussed us at all and instead were having a family visit. Jake and his father were joking about something, and Nathalie was laughing. They looked like a very happy family. With a round of hugs and handshakes Mr. and Mrs. Logan prepared to leave when Nathalie pulled me into a small sitting room off the foyer as the girls stood around chatting with the two Logan men.

"I never got to answer your question," she began once we were in the room. "How I knew."

I nodded, prompting her to go on.

"What Anthony never knew is, while I was clear-headed about everything else in my life, I was muddle-headed when it came to him," she chuckled at her memories. "He kept me on my toes, and I'd melt on the spot every time I saw him, and every time I tried to think about it, try to make the whole thing clear in my head, I managed to get more confused."

Yeah, I knew that feeling.

"One day his mother told me 'don't think about it, just feel it and you'll know.' You're a strong one, Charlene," she said, holding my hands in hers. "I can see that about you. You're smart, and you seem to have a very level head on your shoulders. But with him, don't think about it...just feel it."

She hugged me to her tightly, smelling of warm vanilla and cinnamon. It felt so much like I was hugging my own mom I nearly cried. Over her shoulder I met Jake's gaze as he came searching for his mother, and he paused, smiling at the sight of us before moving back to the foyer.

She held me again at arms length, bringing a hand to cup my cheek. "Just feel it, okay?"

I nodded.

Satisfied that I understood her meaning, she left the sitting room with me just behind her.

"There she is," Anthony said. "You ready?"

Nathalie smiled and hugged Jake. "Yep. See you later, honey. Love you."

"Love you, too, mom," Jake responded, kissing her cheek.

"You ladies be good to him," she ordered as she twined fingers with her husband's and went through the door.

A mere half-hour after they'd gone, we were all back in the living room awaiting the arrival of another guest. Jake strode into the room with a bounce in his step.

"Meeting my parents wasn't so bad, right?" he joked as some of the ladies forced smiles. "All right, the next person I'd like you to meet is someone I've known all my life. He's like a brother to me. Some of you may have heard of him, well-known fashion photographer, Mr. Marcus Broussard."

We all cheered as the man walked through the door. The two men embraced in a bear hug, huge grins on their faces as they spoke with each other quickly. Marcus was a few inches shorter than Jake, with a slightly leaner build and darker mahogany complexion. Physically the two could have really been brothers, and the bond between them was evident.

"Hello," he said in a cheerful voice. "I'm gonna hang out with you for a while so I can get to know you and see which one of you is right for my boy. Sound good?"

"Yeah," we all said together, reminiscent of answering the teacher in first grade.

"Great, so let's all go out to the patio and get some drinks."

A few girls immediately latched on to Jake, guiding him outside. I was bringing up the rear when Marcus grabbed my arm.

"Whoa, whoa, whoa. Aren't you gonna say hi, Char?"

I stared at him blankly then remembered what Char had said. *You don't pass up a Broussard shoot.*

"Of course I was, Marcus," I said, giving him a quick hug, hoping he didn't pick up on my hesitation. "I just didn't want the other girls to think I was a ringer, you know. That I already knew Jake's friends and had an advantage."

Marcus smirked, dark eyes glittering, obviously not buying the bullshit I was selling. "So this is where you've been holed up since Costa Rica, huh?"

"Yeah. Didn't I mention I was coming on here?" His manner was very direct, like he could see right through me, and the feeling made me shiver. This could be trickier than I thought.

He shook his head. "Not once while we were together. Straight up, are you really feelin' Jake?"

In more ways than you know, I thought. "Yeah, Marcus, I really am. He's a great guy. A real sweetheart."

He held up his hands in surrender, a disappointed look on his face. "Okay. I'll back off. But I gotta tell him we know each other. I'm not gonna lie to my family."

My brain was already occupied with trying to tell the man I was falling for that I wasn't who he thought I was. Marcus could tell Jake he was an E-wok for all I cared.

"No need to lie, Marcus. I'm sure Jake understands. Occupational hazard, running into people you worked with," I giggled.

Marcus eyed me suspiciously a while longer then said, "Okay, Char."

We were turning to leave when a voice called to him.

"Marcus! It's been forever," Tamara exaggerated.

I noticed Marcus brace himself for the enthusiastic hug and kiss the woman gave him.

"Tamara," he said, unable to mask the disdain in his voice. "What the *hell* are you doin' here?"

"Getting my man back," she replied assuredly, linking arms with him. "That whole thing—breaking it off with Tank—that was a mistake. I realized how much he meant to me after I left. And," she went on excitedly for my benefit, "from the way he's been acting, I think he missed me, too! It's just a matter of time before we're back together."

I know she was trying to get under my skin, but something about the way she said it, so definitively, made my stomach drop. I knew Jake and I had something special, but then that was the point of this wasn't it? Every girl still here thought she and Jake had something special. She might be his ex, but Tamara was still here.

I excused myself to the patio, leaving Marcus to contend with the production that was starlet Tamara James. This feeling of uncertainty was a new wrench in an already shaky machine. I'd just have to clear it up with Jake…right after I told him I'm not really a model named Charlene. God, what a mess!

I paused when I reached the patio, watching Jake laugh with several of the girls—Tabitha perched on his lap—and for the first time I saw that he might actually have a connection with a few of them. I mean, sure he said some really amazing things yesterday, but in the heat of the moment people are likely to say anything, right? And how did I know he wasn't making everyone here feel the same way or saying the same things? He smiled at me and waved me over, but I just stood there, blinders off. How could I have been stupid enough to think bad boy Jake Logan might have any real feelings for me?

I gave him a weak smile, shaking my head. "I kinda got a headache," I lied.

"Need me to get you something?" A genuinely concerned look was on his face as he started to scoot Tabitha off his lap so he could get up.

"No, no. Go ahead and stay. I'll be okay. Just need to lie down for a minute."

He frowned a moment, then conceded. "I'll check on you in a little while."

I hurried past Tamara and Marcus, who looked like he'd rather put his eyes out with toothpicks than continue talking.

"You okay, Char?" he called as I ascended the stairs.

"How do you two know each other?" Tamara asked suspiciously.

Marcus looked to me and I to him, and we both ignored her question.

"Yeah, Marcus. Just need to lie down. Back in a minute."

I got to my room and threw myself on the bed. Between my feelings for Jake, trying to figure out Jake's feeling's for me, and still needing to tell him I wasn't who he thought I was, I was thoroughly confused.

"Dammit, Charlie," I mumbled into the pillow. "What the hell did you get yourself into?"

Chapter 13

As soon as Marcus left the house several hours later Jake spotted Charlie near the pool and made a beeline toward her.

"We need to talk," he said dryly, gently grasping her elbow.

"Couldn't agree with you more."

"Jacob," Tamara cooed, catching up with the pair and tucking neatly under Jake's free arm. "Come get in the pool with us, baby."

"Give me a minute," he said absently, pulling his arm from her shoulder.

"Aww. Trouble in paradise? Finally figured out she's not the girl you thought she was, Tank? I never did figure out how you and Marcus know each other, Charlene," she sneered.

Jake spun to face her quickly. "Don't call me that ever again, understand?" He shot Tamara a look that would freeze fire then continued to guide Charlie to the other side of the yard.

Tamara glared at their retreating forms, a cocky grin on her face, before spinning on her heel and returning to the group of women by the pool.

With cameramen in tow, Jake and Charlie came to a stop at the low fence that kept people from descending the hill, unintentionally or otherwise. Jake leaned his arms on the rail and looked down the grassy incline while Charlie leaned her back against it, keeping a watchful eye on Amanda who was perched oddly on a barstool.

"What's the matter, Char? Your head still hurting?" he asked sarcastically.

"No."

"Because it never was and you don't lie very well. So what's the problem? Why have you been avoiding me since Marcus got here?" he pressed.

"I'm not avoiding you, Jake."

"No bullshit, no pretense, right Char? Not between you and me. So tell me."

She opened her mouth to speak but, unable to figure out how to voice what was going on in her head, she snapped it shut. And from the look on Jake's face his news couldn't wait.

"You first."

Jake sighed, still staring out in the distance, and shooed a fly away from his face. "Why didn't you tell me you knew Marcus?"

She wasn't expecting that. "Because I didn't know *you* knew Marcus, let alone that he was your best friend. And by the time he'd shown up," she shrugged, "it was all out in the open. We worked the Dolce shoot together. No big deal. Don't tell me you're jealous of your boy?"

"Nah. Why didn't you tell me you *knew* Marcus? In a more...*personal* way?" he asked, turning his head to gage her expression.

The look on Charlie's face went from utter confusion to surprised realization to "aww shit, Char" in a matter of seconds. Now she was truly stuck. This was not the way to tell Jake about everything she was hiding. Once again Char had managed to dig a hole that Charlie would have to climb out of.

"Dammit Char! I'm kickin' your ass when I see you again," she forced through clenched teeth.

Jake frowned, thinking she'd lost it. "What?"

Charlie shook her head, chewing her lip nervously as she ran the different outcomes of the situation through her mind. None of them looked good.

"So now you know what I'm talking about?"

No I don't! she wanted to scream, but what could she do?

"Just how did Marcus say I *knew* him, Jake?" she asked trying to stay calm and gather enough strength to finally clear her conscience.

"Costa Rica. Just a few days before we started taping. He said after your shoot you two went back to your room and he looked after you while you were sick. One thing led to another…a little kissing…a little touching…you recovered from your fatigue pretty quickly, apparently, because you managed to show up here…oh, that you being here explains why you hadn't returned his calls, and that you actually tried to act like you'd never seen him before when he spoke to you in the living room."

Charlie couldn't believe her ears. She'd have to have a serious talk with Char right after that ass kicking.

"He also mentioned you brought your boyfriend with you. Is he the same guy Tamara and I saw with his hands all over you at the club? The one you made me believe was your sister's friend?"

"Did he tell you I slept with him?"

Jake ground his teeth, his features hardening as he strained to keep his voice level. "Did you?"

Charlie ran an exasperated hand through her hair. "Jake, there's something you really need to know."

"Believe me, angel-face, I'm all ears."

She took a deep breath ordering her thoughts in her head. She had one shot at this and couldn't afford to blow it. "First, I don't know Marcus, in any way, shape or form. *Personally* or…impersonally. The first time *I* met him was today when he walked into this house."

"But you did the shoot together?"

"It's complicated."

"Well *un*-complicate it for me, Char," he bit out, a pained look crossing his handsome face.

Charlie couldn't stand it. There was so much to say and none of it seemed like enough to explain away what she and Char had done to him. She was lower than dirt. Than scum. Than…than Tamara.

"My name's not Charlene," she said hurriedly, chewing her lower lip and looking away.

"What?"

She sighed heavily forcing herself to look at him and repeating herself clearly. "My name's not Charlene, Jake."

"Oookaaay," he dragged, looking at her quizzically. "Then what *is* your name?"

She cringed. "Charl—"

"Oh my God!" someone screamed from the other side of the yard.

"—otte," Charlie finished faintly as she spun in the direction of the commotion and saw Amanda sprawled across the stone floor near the bar. "Call an ambulance, Jake. *Now!*" she ordered, kicking off the heels and running over to Amanda who was convulsing on the ground with two girls over her trying to hold her arms and legs. "Just let her seize! Give her room, and someone get a pillow for her head."

Immediately the girls moved back, giving Charlie space to work.

"Who saw what happened?" Charlie asked as Jake came to a halt beside her.

"We were just out here drinking and stuff and then she fell off the chair and started shaking," Tabitha replied timidly, on the verge of tears as her eyes took in the sight of Amanda's jerking body. "Is she gonna be okay?"

"Did she hit her head?"

"Yeah, when she fell, it kinda bounced on the ground."

"How long were you drinking and how much did she drink?" Charlie asked, moving everything away from Amanda as she twitched and convulsed.

"We were doing tequila shots. Like maybe ten or twelve."

"How long?" Charlie pressed in full physician mode.

Tabitha stammered, looking to the other ladies for help. "Uh—umm—maybe fifteen… twenty minutes."

The operator finally came on the phone with Jake. "Yes, my name is—"

Charlie snatched his cell phone as a girl rushed back with a pillow. "This is Dr. Charlotte Roberts, ID number delta gamma gamma eight six five. I'm at three two seven seven Coastline Drive with patient Amanda Sullivan, age twenty-three. Need an ambulance, ASAP. She's currently suffering a seizure probably caused by hyponatremia due to rapid alcohol intake. Possible subdural hematoma and concussion. Patient was treated at Kaiser, Culver City about a month ago for seizure."

Charlie watched as the attack subsided then lifted Amanda's head to slide the pillow under and tilted her on her side. She then noticed Amanda's exposed arm was swelling near the shoulder.

"She may also have suffered a humoral fracture, right side."

She quickly checked Amanda for any other obvious injuries and, noticing none, returned her attention to the phone.

Jake watched with a mixture of awe and concern as everything about him moved in slow motion. What the hell had just happened? Poor Amanda was having a seizure. And *Doctor* Roberts? Doctor *Charlotte* Roberts?

"Hurts so bad," Amanda wailed, tears streaming down her face before she threw up the contents of her stomach.

"You're okay," Charlie soothed, holding her firmly until the deluge of tequila and stomach acid ended, the phone perched between shoulder and ear. She wiped the Amanda's mouth with a paper towel someone handed her from the bar and noticed the woman was trembling, head lolling. "Amanda? Can you hear me?"

Amanda croaked lightly, her eyes fluttering.

"Patient's vomited and is trying to respond. ETA on the medics?"

"Five minutes. I'll stay on the line until they arrive." The operator replied.

Sirens wailed in the distance.

"Anything we can do?" Jake asked, pushing his own thoughts aside for the moment to make sure Amanda would be okay.

"Make sure they can get straight in."

A few less shell-shocked ladies ran to ensure a path was cleared while Charlie took Amanda's pulse. It was frighteningly low, and she bent to listen for Amanda's faint breathing.

Seconds later, the breathing stopped.

* * * *

"She's arresting! Rush those medics!" I barked into the phone, tossing it to Jake and getting Amanda on her back. I tilted back her head, supported her jaw, and listened for even the slightest exhale.

Nothing.

I sealed my mouth to hers—ignoring the tequila aroma—and pinched her nose closed, giving two quick breaths and checking again.

Nothing.

"Ambulance in four," Jake said.

Thirty fast compressions.

Two breaths.

Thirty.

Two.

Thirty.

Two.

This went on for an eternity, and as the medics came through the door minutes later I thought I'd lost her.

They went to work on her immediately, and I moved out of the way, briefly exhausted. Jake stood near me, watching as the techs managed to bring Amanda coughing back to life...again.

Moments later they had her breathing stabilized and an oxygen mask on her face, and I realized who the team was.

"Get an IV in her, slow drip, Scott. Possible fracture right arm, so watch the swelling."

"Sure thing, Charlie," he said, watching as the team wheeled Amanda through the house on a gurney. "She's lucky you were here. A few minutes more... "

"I know," I interrupted, not needing him to voice it. A few more minutes and my friend might have been dead.

Scott looked to my left then back at me, giving me the once over, and then fell into step as we walked briskly after the retreating gurney.

"Thought you were spending your vacation working on your bike, doc. Though you look better in that outfit than covered in motor oil, I'm sure. You attending on this?"

"Yeah," I replied, ignoring his comment and stopping at the door to slide into my sneakers. I saw Tamara glaring at me but really didn't have the time or the patience. A few of the girls were crying and gasping as we exited. No doubt they'd have lots of questions later.

"Your bodyguard coming with you?" Scott asked as we neared the van, and I realized Jake was at my side, jaw set squarely, eyes slightly narrowed. Looking at both men looking at each other, I also realized they were embroiled in some secret war not immediately apparent to us non-simians.

"Pissing contest later guys, the whole gang's invited. I'll make burgers, bring a ruler, and take bets. It'll be all the rage! But emergencies first, okay? And you know better, Scotty."

Scott turned and stalked to the van to monitor his crew. They had an alert Amanda up and in the back in a few seconds, an IV in her left arm.

"If you want to come by Jake, I think she would appreciate it," I said quietly.

He stared at me a moment, a torrent of emotions crossing his face, then turned on his heel and stalked off in the other direction.

Men.

I stood watching as Tamara rushed to Jake's side, mouth going a thousand miles a minute. She turned and threw me her patent wicked grin then wrapped her arms around his waist. I noticed he didn't reciprocate the gesture, but he didn't push her away either. A surge of jealousy tore through me, making my pulse race, but right now I had more pressing issues to tend to. I climbed in the van behind Scott and pulled the door shut.

* * * *

Four hours after arriving at the hospital Amanda's vitals finally stabilized. The amount of alcohol in her body had caused an electrolyte imbalance that triggered the seizure. After administering more IV fluids, her last set of blood work showed that she was starting to move out of the critical stage and back to normal. She was finally getting some sleep, and her mother had come into the room to be with her.

After relaying all the info to the doctor on shift, I pulled the starched white lab coat off and went to the lockers, hanging it opposite the jean shorts and blouse I had worn in. I was presently wearing a nifty set of puke green hospital scrubs and my comfy gray Nikes. Oh, how I'd missed them! Then I gathered what courage I had and went to the lobby to see if Jake had decided to come or not.

The large waiting room was relatively empty. A woman sat at the far end holding her young son in her lap and staring at the TV. Across the room an older man was dozing in his plastic chair. And standing outside was Jake...with Scott? Apparently God *does* have a sense of humor.

I went outside where the sun was hanging low in the sky, and both men turned as I approached. "Pissing contest over? Who won?" I joked.

Neither laughed.

This was gonna be tough.

"You gonna be alright out here, Charlie?" Scott asked, his hands shoved into the pockets of his navy blue uniform pants.

"I'll be fine. Aren't you on duty?"

"Yours was only the second call this shift. Maybe everyone caught on tonight and decided not to be sick."

"Wishful thinking," I smiled, noticing Jake standing rigidly, waiting for Scott to leave so he could strangle me in peace, no doubt. "Can you give us a minute, Scotty?"

His eyes narrowed slightly before nodding. Then he turned to Jake. "If you hurt her, and I mean so much as a single tear, you'll have to deal with me." He stared hard at Jake to drive his point home—impressive considering Jake's height advantage—then went into the hospital.

After Scott had been gone a while I finally spoke. "Amanda's gonna be okay. Her vitals are stable. Bruised but not broken."

"Glad to hear it," Jake started, staring off across the parking lot, arms crossing his chest as he leaned back on his heels. "Scott's very protective of you. Any particular reason?"

"Scotty's had a crush on me since I started working here. I love him like a brother, and that's all it'll ever be. He's harmless."

"Bodily harm is the least of my concerns right now, Char." He sighed and grit his teeth then corrected himself. "Char-*lotte*."

I took a step closer to him and he stiffened. "What do you want me to say, Jake? I'm really sorry, but honestly, apart from my name and occupation, I'm no different than I was six hours ago. Can you at least look at me?"

He slowly turned to face me, visibly straining to remain calm. "Really? Because I think you're wrong, *Charlotte*. Tell me, exactly why did you make up 'Charlene the model'? Your life seems interesting enough."

"I didn't make up Char, Jake. I was trying to tell you everything, but then Amanda had her episode and it all kind of came out at once without giving me time to clarify. I tried telling you yesterday on the boat—"

"But you thought it'd go better if we had sex first?"

"-but I didn't know where to start," I finished.

"I find the *beginning* is always easiest," he retorted.

I know he's upset, but did he have to make this so hard?

"Charlene's my twin sister. *Identical* twins to be exact." I held up my hand, knowing what he was about to say. "I told you she's my younger sister, because technically she is…by eight minutes. Char's a model. Char knows Marcus, and that's the reason Marcus thought he knew me."

"Oh, well that's simple enough," he said sardonically, shifting his shoulders. "So, why didn't your *twin* come on the show? Why did you pretend to be her instead?"

"I really do have a twin, Jake. You can ask Sco—" I paused, seeing the look on his face before suggesting, "-anyone on staff here and they'll tell you. In fact," I chuckled lightly, "you saw her at the club, walking down the hallway from the bathroom…"

A flicker of recognition lit his eyes but he didn't respond.

"Anyhow, she was the one who wanted to be on the show, not me. She landed the D&G shoot in Costa Rica, the one Marcus was working on and they pushed it back a day for the reps to fly in or something, so she asked me to fill in for her again and then we'd switch after—"

"'Again'? You two do this all the time?" he asked incredulously, cutting me off and fixing me with a cold glare.

I shook my head hard and frowned. "God, no! We haven't switched in eons! And we've *never* switched on a guy for this exact reason. The mess it can cause isn't worth it."

"Well color me lucky," he mocked and then prompted, "'Again'?"

I ran a hand through my hair, waiting for a nosey receptionist to go back inside. By tomorrow this entire drama would be retold across the ER if she caught wind of it.

"I was the one who auditioned, not Char. She was coming back from a shoot in Jamaica at the time and was running late."

"So it was you that day, with the story, and the shirt?" he asked, a little of his anger ebbing. "Kassiwi passego, right? Couldn't get that out of my head."

"You saw the tape?"

"Yeah, I watched the tape. Several times, actually," he admitted with a smirk, his eyes on mine. "But I was there. I came in the middle of that casting, and you were the first girl I saw. I knew I wanted you then. I was gonna back out of the show until I saw you, Charlene. Shit!" he groaned, the frustration returning, arms spread wide before dropping them dejectedly. "That's not even your name! When were you gonna switch? When was the real Charlene gonna come to the house?"

Might as well get it all out on the table.

"Can we sit down?" I asked, walking to a bench. Jake joined me, putting as much space between us as possible on the five-foot seat. "It was supposed to be after the first challenge, the trivia challenge, but the date was in Carmel, so obviously we couldn't do it. The next real opportunity was at the club."

"Which is where I saw you with that guy—"

"Char's agent Tyler. The one Marcus thought was her boyfriend."

"Why? Why did you wanna switch? Why was Char coming to the house in the first place?"

There was no way to say this without hurting him, and as much as it killed me, I had to do it fast like yanking off a band-aid. "Tyler told her coming on the show would get her exposure and help her career take off."

"And Amanda? This is how you really know her…from the hospital?"

"She had an episode the weekend before she went to the show. When we saw each other she begged me not to say anything that would get her sent home, and I asked her not to say anything about me being a doc, so when you came up the stairs that first day she said I was her sitter."

Jake bobbed his head slightly, taking it all in. He was silent a long time, and when he spoke again his voice was hushed. "Were you really just gonna walk away from me like there was nothing between us?"

I nodded slowly, the full weight of it all crashing on my shoulders.

"Why, angel-face?" he breathed.

"Loyal to a fault, Logan," I answered quietly. "Char needed me, and I put myself in a position where her needs had to come before my wants. I didn't want to do it from the start, but I figured in three days I'd be in and out and no one would be the wiser. I didn't go into this expecting us to have a connection, but we did, and I'm really glad we did. I'm sorry you were hurt in all of this and I really hope you can forgive me, Jake."

He dropped his head, chuckling as he stared at the ground between his legs. "Boy, Jake, you did it again," he murmured.

I grabbed his hand, surprised he let me, and pressed it in mine. "Jake, I know there's not much I can say, but I—"

"But what, Charlotte?" he asked, eyes glittering as they searched my face.

I swallowed my words and stared at him conflicted.

We sat in silence a moment before he finally stood up and pulled me with him, hugging me tightly. He put his lips to my temple and held my head to his shoulder. "I'll never find another woman like you," he whispered.

Relief washed over me as I slid my arms around him, holding him close, hearing the steady beat of his heart, inhaling his scent—secure in the knowledge that everything would be okay. That we'd get through this somehow. He pulled back a bit then cradled my face in his large warm hands, holding me gently as he pressed his lips to mine.

When we released each other I looked up into his deep brown eyes, but what I saw wasn't happiness or joy or forgiveness. I saw heartbreak—raw, red, and exposed.

And that's when I knew.

"Sorry, angel-face."

He walked away.

Silent tears spilled down my cheeks, and a sob swelled in my chest. The blood thundered through my veins, and everything in my heart was telling me to go after him. Stop him. Make him understand. But my head wouldn't let me. I just stood there, watching him leave.

I love him.

It's finally crystal clear and I was ready to admit it, but it doesn't really matter now, does it?

I love him, but I hurt him, so I had to let him go. He deserved so much better than what he'd gotten.

He deserved better than me.

But, god, the pain! It's the kind of concentrated heartache that settles deep in your heart, in your bones, wraps itself around you, and crushes all desire to love again. There's no medicine for pain this all-consuming. And that's probably because, when it hurts this bad, you just go numb.

By the time Logan was out of sight, I couldn't feel a thing.

Chapter 14
{*Four Months Later*}

It was just another day here in sunny LA. Well, it was a sunny *autumn* day, although you can't tell because LA doesn't get seasons. Well, it's not that it doesn't get seasons, it's that they just come and go and they all pretty much look the same. Char and I were doing some much needed fall cleaning, because our house looked like the Big One had hit it. Actually, *two* big ones had. Between the both of us and our hectic careers, neither of us were home much to make sure the place sparkled. So on this rare weekend when we were both off we decided to tend to domestic affairs.

We cleaned the major parts of the house together then split up to clean our own rooms. By the time I was done with mine, Char looked as though she'd gotten through a third of hers. Clothes were strewn across every conceivable piece of furniture, and there was a shirt actually hanging from her ceiling fan!

"Need some help?"

"Yes, lawd! How did this place get so messy?" Char asked.

"You always were the messy one, Char." I smiled, pulling a pile of clothes out of an overflowing suitcase. "I'll hang these, assuming they're clean."

She cautiously sniffed a shirt and cringed. "Maybe we should just wash it all to be on the safe side."

I laughed, gathering up clothes from every nook and cranny in her room—and I do mean nook and cranny. Things were shoved beneath her bed, behind her dresser, under the desk.

"The upside to being a model is all the free fashion. The downside is all the free fashion," she chuckled before a theatrical, "My closet runneth over!"

I dropped them in front of her and she set about separating her clothes into piles.

"Anything else I can do?"

"Vacuum."

"This is oddly reminiscent of younger days," I joked.

"Well you offered. When have you known me to pass up free labor?" She took her piles to the laundry room and I ran the vacuum across the floor.

"What else?" I asked when she came back. "Let's speed this up. I'm starving."

"Grab one of those two junk drawers and dump it on my bed."

I pulled the first drawer from the chest and upturned it, pouring out an assortment of old electronic plugs, a flashlight, batteries, gum, and scraps of paper.

"The other one's not your naughty drawer is it?" I asked, half joking.

"Eww, I don't have a naughty drawer, Charlie. But now I know *you* do. Gross!" she squealed, just like when we were kids, before walking out of the room again. It was fun kidding around with her like this. I felt like I hadn't laughed in ages.

I grabbed the second drawer and dumped it. A load of items tumbled out, but my eyes were drawn to only one—the magazine that Char had shown me with the crease down the center keeping the page open.

I carefully picked it up like it was a stone tablet delivered straight from God. STARLET DROPS BAD BOY screamed from the page. The editors had taken a picture of Logan and Tamara exiting one of his nightclubs and created a rip between them, the torn edges to indicate the breakup. I had only glanced at the picture when Char had first shown it to me almost six months ago, taking in the physical, noting how sexy Jake was. Studying his face now, I saw something I hadn't seen there before. There was loneliness in Logan's eyes. Sure he was smiling, but there was emptiness behind it. My mind drifted to the last time I'd seen him and, after four months of forgetting, the pain started just as fresh as the day it happened.

"I'll pay you in lemonade!" Char's happy voice hovered somewhere on the edge of my consciousness, but I was standing outside of the hospital, watching Logan walk away from me all over again.

"Charlie?"

My vision cleared and the magazine rematerialized in my hand. I didn't realize I had been caressing his photo with my fingertip, or that tears had trailed down my cheeks. Char hugged me, sitting me down amidst the pile of junk on her bed.

"It's okay, sweets," she soothed. "It's all right."

No sobs came. No more tears either. And after a moment I was okay. I handed the magazine to Char and tried to stand up, but she forced me back down on the bed.

"I've let you go through this by yourself long enough, Charlie. You haven't said a word about it since it happened. Let it out."

"That's just it, Char. I don't have anything left. I've cried. I've sobbed. I've taken double shifts so I could stay busy, and for what? All I got was a headache."

"You have to do something about it then, Charlie. You need to talk to him, make him forgive you."

"If he wanted to forgive me, he would have. He has my number, and he certainly knows where I work," I said lightly. "There's nothing I can say or do that can make him change his mind, so what's the use?"

"You know that story you used to tell me, about Igrár and the princess? You never told the whole story."

Where was she going with this? "Yes I did. Their daughter comes in, Igrár understands that he passed the impassable test; yadda, yadda, yadda; they live happily ever after. The end." Wherever she was going, God bless her. It was taking my mind off Logan.

Char shook her head, the soft curls that had escaped her ponytail fluttering about her face. "That's not how it ends, sweets. Mom told us the end once, but whenever you told it to me you always thought I'd fallen asleep, so you'd stop at the part with the eyes. There's more than that."

"I'm waiting with bated breath," I smiled.

Her voice dropped into 'fairytale' mode, all wispy and magical. I think she enjoyed finally being on this end of things, so I gave her my full attention.

"Shortly after they were reunited, Igrár became very ill from his many travels to distant lands across the seas. He had the 'sickness' and was kept away from the rest of the village. Still, the princess would go to him, because she loved him so much. On his final day beneath his final moon, chief Sougmou came to see him.

"'My son' he said. 'I am saddened to tell you the Wise Ones do not think you will make it through the night. I only wish I let you be kassiwi passego when you first asked. Now my daughter will know much sadness again.'

"Igrár, struggling to breathe, spoke so softly the chief had to bend to hear him. 'Sougmou, you honor me with your words, and I have known great happiness here. I have seen many lands and known the love of family and friends. There is no reason to regret a thing, for you are a man of your word. I am lucky to have passed the test you gave me.'

"Sougmou shook his head, his eyes sad. 'I am a blind man, Igrár. I should have known before the test that you had given my daughter something far more important than your eyes. You gave her your heart.'"

We sat silently for a moment. I have no idea if that's how my mom ended the story—and I'd never know—but I got Char's point.

"See, sweets," she said. "It doesn't matter if you were pretending to be me. You gave him *your* heart."

I smiled at her sadly, wishing it were that simple. "The eternal problem with fairy-tales, Char. They're not real." I stood from her bed and went to my room. I needed some air.

Thirty minutes and a hot shower later Char had gone through the drawers and gathered all her trash. She'd pulled the bags to the front door and then came barreling out of her room, clothes changed, hair done, and makeup fresh.

"Feeling better?" she asked, knowing I didn't want to talk about it.

"Yeah. We're goin'out to eat? Give me fifteen minutes to shower and change." I turned to go to my room.

"Give me an hour or so, sweets. I just remembered I owe a friend a favor."

She darted out the door before I had a chance to ask if I could help.

* * * *

Charlene marched into the restaurant where Jake and Marcus were having a drink. Seeing Jake in person for the first time she thought she'd be a blubbering fool, because the man was truly attractive and she could see why Charlie was so drawn to him. But seeing Marcus again was another story entirely. She had to keep herself from liquefying on the spot the man was so utterly gorgeous.

She remembered their brief moments together in Costa Rica. After shooting, Tyler had gone off to a club, and she went back to her room feeling absolutely horrible. It was Marcus who'd brought her something to eat and made her tea in ninety-degree weather because her throat was hurting. It was Marcus who'd kissed her, then held her while they watched movies until she fell asleep. And it was Marcus who made her finally realize Tyler didn't deserve her.

Still, Char was here to clear up the mess she'd made, and she had to do it before she could talk to Marcus. As she approached their table both men looked up. Marcus was expecting Charlie, so his look was more of wonder than surprise. But Jake was shocked and something else. Angry? Relieved? Char couldn't fully decipher his expression, so she'd have to tread lightly. Except that's what Charlie would do, and that was the exact reason Charlie *wasn't* here. Charlie had spent the last four months treading lightly. Time to stomp.

"Hi, Marcus," she said briefly before turning to Jake. "Could you excuse us a moment?"

"Charlotte?" Marcus asked, standing so she could sit down. "You and your sister really are exact. I'd swear you were Charlene."

Char tensed. No way he could know her from Charlie. They'd spent less than three days together six months ago. "No. I'm Charlie," she assured with a chuckle, taking the seat he'd vacated. "Don't feel bad, though. I get that a lot."

Jake stared at her, his eyes narrowing a millimeter before returning to normal.

"Well, I'm sure you two need to talk, so I'll just be over there," Marcus said, walking toward the bar.

When they were alone Charlene took a deep breath and went for it. "Jake, how long are we gonna keep this up, huh? Tell me you didn't feel anything for me when we were in that house and I'll leave you alone and won't look back."

"I'm not the one who made contact," he replied dryly. "Why are you here, Char?"

"Charlie," she corrected patiently. "And what brought me here is I'm tired of living like this. It's been four months, Jake! I know what Char and I did was wrong, and I know sorry isn't enough, but what I feel for you is real, Jake. It wasn't for the show, and I think you know that."

Jake leaned back in his chair, grabbing his drink and taking a long swallow. Then he returned the glass to the table and continued staring.

"Dammit, Jake, say something," Char demanded.

He turned his attention to the tablecloth, absently drawing circles with a fingertip, trying to figure out how to handle this situation. Finally he spoke.

"Did she put you up to this?"

Char frowned. "Who?"

"I know you're not Charlotte."

"Jake, it's me! It's Charlie!" she protested.

He shook his head slowly. "No, you're not. You're Char...The *real* Char. If you want to keep this up I'm free most of the day, but I know you're Charlene."

Char's lips turned up slightly at the corners, dropping the charade. "What gave me away?"

"I know every curve of her face, every fleck in her eyes, and every inflection in her voice. You two are nearly exact, but Charlie's eyes are lighter, and she's got a little freckle right about here," he said, reaching out to gently graze Char's face beneath her left eye, his hand dropping before he touched her, pain marring his features as he remembered the woman he loved. His voice softened, "And angel-face calls me Logan. It would have been the first thing she said when she came in."

Char leaned back in her chair and exhaled heavily, raking her fingers through her hair. "Okay, Jake. Hear me out. You and *angel-face* are being ridiculous. In four months she's done nothing but think of you. She hears your name and melts. She saw your picture today and nearly cried! The woman is crazy about you! And from the sound of it you still feel something for her. This whole thing is my doing; so if you wanna blame someone, blame me. Charlie would never have tried to deceive you if not for me."

"Loyal to a fault," he said, his voice a hollow echo. "Part of me is glad you guys did it, because bein' with her was..." He swallowed his words and pulled himself together, his voice firming. "Why isn't she here instead of you?"

Charlene's eyes softened along with her voice. "It's not her way, Jake. She knows you were hurt in this mess and doesn't want to force you. Charlie's always been like that. She'd rather be miserable herself than to be happy and make someone she loves miserable in the process. And she does love you, Jake; make no mistake about that. So please, be mad at me, not her."

Jake chuckled mirthlessly. "You know, I wish I *were* mad. Mad is simple. I know what to do with anger." He paused as though mulling it over, his fingers again drawing circles on the tablecloth. "Sorry, Char. The damage is done."

"You're afraid, aren't you? Not of being hurt, but of loving her that deeply?" She pulled his hand from the table and clasped it in both of hers, forcing him to look at her. "Do you now how amazing it is to find someone to trust your heart to completely?"

"And look where that got me, Char? She hurt me!" he growled, finally voicing the pain he'd kept bottled up for so long. "The cut's too deep."

Charlene shook her head, tears welling in her eyes. "*I* hurt you. I hurt *both* of you. And for that I am so, so sorry. Saying it a thousand times wouldn't make it up to you. I love my sister more than anything, Jake, and I'm sure I've hurt her in the past. But this..." she trailed off, unable to keep the tears from falling. Her voice cracked as she continued. "I don't know how she ever found it in her heart not to blame me for this, but she doesn't, 'cause that's how Charlie is. I've never seen her so unhappy. I don't know you, but seeing the same pain on your face, hearing it in your voice...and knowing I'm the cause of heartache for two wonderful people who obviously belong together is unbearable. So that's why I'm here, Jake. To try to repair the damage I've done to you both. Please let me do that."

Jake pulled his eyes from hers, knowing Char was being sincere but too overcome by his own pain and the intensity of the situation to respond. After a while Char released his hand and stood to leave, wiping her eyes with her fingertips.

"If you change your mind Marcus knows how to reach me. Sorry again, Jake." She stopped briefly to say goodbye to Marcus and left.

"That was Charlene?" Marcus chuckled as he reached the table, eyes glued to her retreating form until she disappeared behind the doors.

Jake nodded, deep in thought. Seeing her dredged up pain he'd worked hard to move past. Seeing Charlene reminded him how much he still loved Charlotte.

"Those two are definitely a handful."

"You knew she was coming?" Jake asked detached, still staring off into space.

"Correction, I knew *Charlotte* was coming. I had nothing to do with Charlene showing up, although I wish she'd have stayed longer. She's been keeping her distance since this show debacle. You're blockin' my action, J," he joked, taking his seat and setting his glass on the table.

Jake didn't respond, just dropped his eyes to stare at the tablecloth.

"You're in bad shape, man," Marcus noted and then exhaled heavily, "but I did say you were a masochist. You're doing this to yourself, y'know."

"You seem to be an expert on the situation, Mark. Please. Enlighten me," Jake replied evenly, wondering why his best friend was being so damn chipper about the circumstances.

Marcus took a swallow of his drink and leaned back in his chair. "J, I've known you, what, thirty-two... thirty-three years? Pretty much all your life, right?"

"Correction, I'm three months older than you, so technically I've know you all *your* life."

"And in all that time I've never seen you this crazy over a girl."

"What about Karla McIntire."

"Third grade doesn't count."

"I was gonna marry that girl," Jake sighed wistfully with a little grin.

"She ate paste!" Marcus laughed, shaking his head. "Okay, a girl out of a training bra with a *slightly* more refined palate."

"What about Tamara?" Jake challenged, raising a brow.

"Nah, Tamara *drove* you crazy. There's a difference. Y'know, you could have any girl you want any time you want. You're Jake Logan! Rich playboy nightclub owner! You don't go to the party. You *are* the party! Girls would sell their mothers to date you," Marcus announced theatrically.

"Bit excessive, don'tcha think?"

"But this woman Charlotte, she's got you here," Marcus said sincerely, tapping a finger to his head, "and she's got you here," he finished, tapping over his heart. "That's a rare combination, Jacob."

"How can I trust her? How do I know that what she felt on the show wasn't an act?"

"J, why did you go on the show? You ever come up with that answer?"

"Spite," he bit out, brushing invisible lint from his pants with the back of his hand.

"Who? You're parents?" Marcus shook his head. "You're bigger than that, J."

Jake conceded with a sigh. "I went on the show for her, all right? The day I saw her at the audition I was drawn to her, wanted to know more about her. I figured, two months in a house with her..."

"Aha!" Marcus exclaimed, slapping his palm on the table like he'd made an important discovery. "So you got what you wanted! Now, since her name and job are different, does that mean you don't want her anymore? A rose by any other name, Jake."

They sat in silence, watching as waiters moved about delivering meals to hungry patrons. One approached their table, but Marcus waved him off.

"You're in love with her," he said plainly. "And you're trying to solve a matter of the heart with your head. That's not how it works."

Jake bobbed his head. "But Charlie didn't show up here today, did she?"

"Apparently she's as bullheaded as you are—or as masochistic—so Charlene came to tell you what Charlotte couldn't. You had the poor woman in tears, which I didn't appreciate by the way, but I'll let it slide under the circumstances." Marcus took another swallow of his drink and continued. "Did you stop to consider that, even though they had the chance to switch at the club, they didn't?"

Jake scrubbed his hand over his face as realization dawned. He hadn't even considered that fact. There must have been a reason they didn't switch. They certainly had enough time that night. He stored that info in his mind and continued to let his bruised ego convince him Charlotte didn't care about him one iota.

"Don't you think if she felt anything for me she'd have fought a little harder?"

"Felt anything? Fought harder! Tamara screwed you over, made you out to be a horrible cheat when you dumped her, fought her way back into your life by way of the show—undoubtedly for her own personal gain—and I know the only thing she feels for you is that you're her meal ticket. On the other hand, Charlie comes on the show—"

"Posing as her model sister who needs exposure," Jake interjected.

Marcus rolled his eyes at the interruption and continued, "-Falls in love with you, and then when she realizes how badly she hurt you, loves you enough to let you go. I'd say she feels a hell of a lot for you, bro. Oh, and I'll add that ER doc is *much* more ambitious than gold digger.

"Listen, J, Charlene tried to use your show to get ahead. Not the nicest thing, but not punishable by death. Charlotte, on the other hand, couldn't do it, and apart from her name and occupation you got to know the real Charlie. Now if you'd rather sit here and live it up at your own pity party, be my guest. I'll have balloons and streamers brought in and you can grumble and gripe all you want. But I believe it was Dietrich who said 'grumbling is the death of love'." Marcus downed the last of his drink and returned the empty glass to the table.

Jake smirked, muttering, "I really hate it when you're my conscience."

"It's a dirty job, Jake." Marcus went on cheerfully, fingering the scrap of paper Charlene had handed him. "So, am I calling an event planner, or…"

Chapter 15

After throwing out the trash from our cleaning endeavor (leave it to Char to bail midway) and taking a hot shower, my nerves were still frazzled and I desperately needed to get out of the house. Seeing Jake's picture in that magazine sent me into a tailspin and open road was in order. Char had left almost three hours ago and I figured she probably needed more time with her friend, so a quick ride down the coast would get me back here before dinner. I pulled on my jeans, black boots, and a thick blue hooded sweatshirt over my tee shirt, and went to the front closet. I put on my leather riding jacket and scooped up my keys and lid from the table by the door, the cordless phone in my hand so I could tell my sister I'd be back in a little while, when Char came through the door with her makeup a wreck. Char's makeup was never a wreck. It was flawless even when she was sick!

"What happened? Why were you crying?" I asked, dropping my keys and helmet and following her to the bathroom where she began scrubbing her face.

"Did Tyler do something to you? If he hurt you I'll kill him."

"Charlie, I haven't seen Tyler since that night at the Red Room," she said, lathering her face with soap. "And before that not since Costa Rica."

Where've I been? Oh, right.

"What happened?"

"With Tyler? Let's just say I finally saw him for the—what is it you called him?—self-serving, vile, disgusting, lying cheat without half the wits God gave a slug, insufferable jackass he is."

"That slug part was all you, but it's fitting." I joked.

"Well, you were right. I wanted more. Just not with Tyler." She dried her face, looking refreshed, though her eyes were still a little pink. "You can do your victory dance now."

I stored her comment for later, 'cause that was definitely reason to celebrate. "So what's the matter then? Who or what has you crying? Should I put on my ass-kickin' boots?"

Without warning she hugged me tightly. "I'm so sorry, Charlie."

"For what? What's wrong, Char?" I hugged her back, fearing the worst.

She released me then dropped her eyes to the floor. "I really screwed things up for you and Jake. So I saw him today to try to talk to him."

"You what?" God save me! I'm gonna kill her!

"Charlie, let me explain—"

"No, Char! Please tell me you didn't do that. Tell me you're joking." I turned from her and stomped to the living room, plopping down on the couch.

"Listen, Charlie," she said, sliding onto the seat next to me. "He had to know how you feel. I had to do something for hurting you the way I did. I know you love him, and because of me you two aren't together."

"Char, I've spent the last four months forgetting Logan. I'm over him, okay? You didn't have to go down there to fix anything 'cause nothing was broken. Everything is the way it should be."

Char was silent a minute and I could feel her studying me. "You don't always have to be strong, Charlie. Those eight minutes made you older than me, so you've always been the big sister helping out your little sister. No matter what the little sister does, the big one ends up getting her out of a jam. But sometimes the little sister has to help the big sister out. And that's what I tried to do today."

"Well, thank you, Char," I managed, still fuming but knowing she had good intentions. "But, honestly, everything's okay. I'll be okay. *I* screwed things up with Jake, not you. I could have told him before everything hit the fan, but I didn't. So it's my fault, not yours."

"Wanna know what he said?"

I was dying to hear it.

"No. Maybe someday, way, way, *way* down the line. But not today." I hopped up, grabbed my lid and keys and headed for the door. "I'm gonna go for a ride. Be back in a little while. Dinner when I get back?"

"Sure," Char beamed dragging a hand through her curly tresses. "I'll make reservations at Sticky Rice."

"Sounds good." I reached for the door handle and stopped. "Forgot my license." I returned the items to the table and went back to my room to rummage through my purse, fishing out my license, cash, and cell phone and shoving them into the pocket in my jacket lining. I heard the doorbell ring as I switched off the radio. "You having company?" I called, hearing the door open.

I didn't get a response.

"Char." I said, coming down the hall and back into the living room where Marcus and Char stood talking. He turned as I entered the space, stared at me, spun back to Char quickly, then back to me again.

"Jeez, it's hard to tell you two apart," he chuckled, reaching out his hand. "We were never formally introduced, Charlotte. Marcus Broussard."

"Nice to see you again, Marcus." I shook his hand and grinned, noticing Char was smiling her face off in the background and doing a silly little happy dance that mirrored the one I always do in my head. So he's the reason Tyler's gone. God bless him. By all accounts Marcus was a decent guy and if he made my sister smile, he was cool by me. "Call me Charlie. I was just going for a ride so I'll leave you alone."

"You two even *sound* exactly alike," he chuckled in amazement then said lower, "My boy never knew what hit him."

I let his comment pass, not wanting to ruin the evening for Char or start crying. I glanced back at her and cocked a brow. "I'll assume I'm on my own for dinner, so I'll get something while I'm out. Have fun you two."

I grabbed my gear again and started for the door when Jake walked through it, stopping me in my tracks. "Logan?" For a split second I was breathless and elated, taking in the sight of him in a fitted brown sweater, light blue jeans, brown boots and a chocolate colored leather jacket. He looked every bit as handsome as the last time I'd seen him, and my heart started racing.

Then I remembered what happened the last time I'd seen him and frowned. He wasn't smiling or anything. In fact, he looked as uncertain about being here as I was about his being here. The adrenaline in my blood was now fueling a different kind of fire. "What the hell are you doing here?" I asked gruffly.

"Hello to you, too, *doctor* Roberts," he replied tersely, stopping a few feet from me.

"If my presence upsets you then why are you at *my* house?" I asked, rolling my eyes. "You know what? Stay. I was on my way out anyhow. Then you won't be upset anymore, 'kay?"

Now *I* was upset.

Upset that he could make me upset.

Upset that Char had poked this hornet's nest and once again I was being stung.

Upset that…that…that I'd lied to myself, because after four months I still had feelings for this man.

I moved to go around him and he moved closer to block my exit, holding up his hands.

"Charlie, don't go. Look, I'm sorry, it's just…" he exhaled struggling for words, his voice and eyes softening. "Can we talk?"

I noticed that was the first time he'd called me Charlie, and I liked the way he said it. Nonetheless, I kept my derisive tone. "Oh, I thought we cleared up everything when you left me at the hospital. There's nothing left to say. Let's just move on, 'kay?" Damn these infernal tear ducts! I turned toward the kitchen so he couldn't see my face and quickly swiped my hand across my eyes.

"You know I don't like when you ride upset, sweets," Char said from across the room.

I turned around, eyes dry as the Mojave. "Upset? What makes you think I'm upset, Char?" I smiled brightly.

She gave me her 'don't even try to bullshit me' look—face distorted with one brow in a stern frown, the other cocked slightly, gray eyes narrowed, lips pursed tightly, hands on her hips. She looked just like mom whenever we got caught in a lie.

"Whose side of this are you *on*?" I groaned even though I knew she was right. In my present emotional state there's no way I could safely ride my bike. I probably couldn't even walk down the street straight at this point.

Char didn't budge, so I caved, tossing my helmet and keys back on the table with a loud clatter. "Fine. Let's get this over with, Jake," I said, slipping out of my jacket and plopping down on the loveseat, crossing my arms.

"Jake? You can do better than that," he said lightly. He pulled off his coat and took a seat on the couch across from me.

"What's the difference? It's your name, and right now I can think of a few choice words to call you that are *far* less appealing than 'Jake'."

"Play nice, Charlie," Char admonished sweetly.

"I know where you sleep, Char," I retorted in the same singsong voice.

Marcus snickered.

"On that note, she's all yours, Jake," Char said, grabbing her bag and Marcus's hand, rushing him out the door and closing it quickly behind them.

We sat in silence a moment, looking for something to say. He shifted to the edge of the couch, spreading his bent knees wide, leaning forward and propping his elbows on them.

"How've you been, Charlie?"

"Never better," I deadpanned.

He looked around spotting my helmet on the table. "Going for a ride to make the world okay?"

"My world's fine, Jake," I replied deliberately, an edge to my tone. "Or at least it was before Char decided to contact you. Wasn't yours?"

"No," he said softly, brown eyes boring into mine.

I swallowed hard, trying to force some anger back into my voice but failing. "Exactly what did she tell you when she saw you today?"

"Actually, she tried to be you," he chuckled lightly, that familiar easy grin on his face.

My mouth dropped open in shock. "Char told you she was me?"

Jake nodded, eyes glittering with amusement. "Marched into the restaurant on a mission. Said if I didn't feel anything for her she'd leave without looking back."

"The woman's certifiable!" I giggled, shaking my head. You can't pull a double switcheroo. That's just unheard of. "Did you think she was me?"

"I know you Charlie. You've got lighter eyes and the beauty mark, for starters. But your energies aren't the same. Char's energy is kind of impulsive and frenetic where yours is more practical and calming. You could have a hundred identical sisters and I'd pick you out of a lineup every time. You look the same, but you're completely different shades of gray, y'know?"

Impressive. He'd figured out in a few months what it took most people years. I tried to ignore the melting going on in the pit of my stomach, but I couldn't. "So what got you to come here then?"

"Well," he began casually, "after she admitted being Charlene, she told me everything you told me; that it was her idea and she's really sorry that I was hurt in the process—and I *was* hurt, Charlie."

"I'm sorry, Jake. I never meant—"

"That when you saw my picture today you nearly cried," he continued, holding up a hand to halt another useless apology. "But Char told me something else, too." He paused, staring me in the eyes, his voice turning serious. "That you still have feelings for me, Charlotte."

"She what?" I asked evenly, my face blank. You know, being an only child might not be so bad. And if prison food is anything like hospital food I'm sure I'll manage. My voice turned contemplative. "Think a judge will buy justifiable homicide? 'Cause I'm gonna strangle Char. Slowly."

"Don't be mad at her, angel-face," he said in that deep velvet voice.

Char's voice intruded on my musings. *You don't always have to be strong, Charlie.* Then Nathalie Logan's voice followed. *Don't think; just feel.* I reluctantly admitted they were both right.

I let out a frustrated sigh, wiping my hands down the sides of my face. "I'm not mad at her. Her heart's in the right place even if her head isn't."

"Then don't be mad at me. I shouldn't have just walked away from you like that, but given the circumstances—"

"I'm not mad at you either, Jake," I interrupted softly, raking my hand through my hair. "I'm mad at myself. I should have told you the truth before things got...even more complicated. Before..."

"Before we made love?" he offered, cocking a brow.

I nodded, grinning sheepishly, my brain picking the worst possible moment to replay the details. I refocused my attention on Jake's face, which didn't help all that much. "That wasn't fair to you. You went into it thinking I was someone I wasn't."

"It wasn't all on you, Charlie. I wasn't exactly trying to stop anything that happened on the boat," he said with a smirk.

I put my face into my hands. "Regardless, I really made a mess of everything, Jake, and I'm really sorry. I just want you to forgive me."

"When we were at the hospital, I couldn't believe what was happening. I kept hoping it was a horrible nightmare and I would wake up any second on that boat with you curled up beside me. When I got back to the house and all the other girls kept asking what happened to Amanda and to you, I couldn't handle it." He stared at the floor between his knees, his voice cracking slightly. "I was completely numb, Charlie."

I knew that feeling all too well.

His statement hung in the air for a stretch, and I could see the litany of emotions crossing his face. I had to break the silence, the question burning at the back of my brain for months finally surfacing.

"So what happened to the girl you chose, Jake?" I asked quietly.

He lifted his gaze and his brows to me in response.

"Was it Nicole? Or did you get back with Tamara? She did say it was only a matter of time before you two reunited."

"If it matters, I stopped taping. We never finished the show."

"Why not?" I frowned trying to hide my relief.

"Because my heart wasn't in it, Charlie," he answered quickly then redirected the subject. "Listen, I didn't give you the chance to explain everything at the hospital, and I'm sorry for that. You weren't the only one at fault that day. And I know there are a lot of things we probably need to talk about and clear up. But answer this for me first. Why didn't you and Char switch at the club that night?"

I studied his stormy face a minute, seeing that this was something he really needed to know and realizing it was time to get everything off my chest. My heart started racing the way it does when you're about to lay everything on the line and pray you don't get rejected, and that's probably because I was.

"'Cause I was falling for you," I said meeting his eyes. "The night on the roof, all I could think about was how nice it would be to watch every sunset with you, and wake up to you every morning. And how much I wanted you to know the truth about me and Char. I tried to pull away from you, to protect you from me, but I couldn't 'cause...

"And at the hospital I wanted to tell you how I felt so badly, but it wouldn't have been fair to you or me. I didn't want you to think I'd only said it to smooth things over between us, so I had to respect your decision and let you go." I paused, inhaling deeply to get my fluttering pulse under control. "We didn't switch because I'm in love with you, Logan. You already had my heart."

Silence.

I'd made my ardent admission and was met with silence. My ears went fuzzy from the deafening quiet; the only sound I could make out was my heart shattering all over again. My pulse thundered through my veins, kicking into high gear like I had run uphill. I guess in a way I had.

"Come here, Charlie," he finally said, standing and reaching out his hand to me. I pulled myself out of the seat and crossed the space that separated us. Putting my hand in his, he pulled me close, placing both my arms around his neck and his arms around my waist. Being this close to him again, inhaling his scent, feeling his warmth, was everything I thought I'd never experience again. He bent his forehead to mine, the familiarity of the intimate act making my eyes close.

"I missed you so much, angel-face," he whispered. "I meant it when I said I'd never find another woman like you. There's no one like you, not even your twin. You're smart, strong, independent, beautiful, considerate, and funny...and everything I've ever looked for in a woman. I'm lucky to have ever met you, and I love you with every fiber of my being." He paused then said sadly, "I only regret you didn't tell me how you felt four months ago."

Here it comes. This is the part where he leaves me all over again. I braced myself for impact, willing my legs to keep me upright and my eyes to hold back the torrent of tears welling up behind them. I was subconsciously holding my breath and had to make a concerted effort to perform the usually involuntary process.

I felt one of his arms leave my waist, deciding that whoever said lightning didn't strike the same place twice had never had their heart broken. Waiting for his other arm to move and for him to leave me was a reality I'd already experienced once, and it was more than enough the first time. But if he didn't want me, I'd have to deal with it... again.

I felt his body moving from mine, my arms sliding from his neck to his shoulders and lowering slowly in front of my body, but I couldn't open my eyes; didn't want to see him go again. The arm that remained around my waist tightened and he pulled my middle to his chest. I realized he was still with me and slowly opened my eyes.

"Doctor Charlotte Roberts," he said hoarsely, looking up at me from bended knee. "Will you marry me?"

Silence.

He'd just proposed to me, made *his* ardent admission, and I was so surprised all I could give him was silence.

I shook my head slightly, which he must have mistook for my answer because a defeated look crossed his gorgeous face, and I forced the sound around my thudding heart which had lodged itself in my throat. "Wait! Not *no*. That's not what I'm saying. I mean—I—uh—you...Are you sure?"

"Charlie, listen, I understand why you did what you did for Char. I'd do anything for my family, too. But I haven't stopped thinking about you or loving you since I first saw you, baby. I let my pride get in the way before. I'd be a fool to let you go again."

I looked at him, trying to be sure this is what he wanted to do, 'cause lord knows I did. "But—uh—do you...Can you forgive me?"

"Still trying to protect me from you, huh?" He chuckled low and cocked a brow. "I'm proposing to you, angel-face. I think it's safe to assume I forgive you. So..."

I smiled so hard I thought my face would crack. Then I nodded so hard I thought my head would fall off.

"Yes?"

"Yes! God, yes! I'll marry you, Logan!"

He pressed his head to my belly, hugging me tightly, and I could hear the smile in his low voice. "I love you so much, angel-face."

"I love you, too, Jake." I pressed my lips to the crown of his head, clutching him to me.

We stayed that way for a while then he finally stood from the floor, drawing me back into his arms and lifting me as we kissed. God, I'd missed the taste of him in my mouth, his strong arms wrapped around me, and I smiled at the thought that I'd have this every day for the rest of my life.

When he put me down and we separated, he held out the ring that was in his hand. I'd been so surprised I hadn't even noticed it. I finally focused on it, hearing Gary the salesman's French-accented English description of the Yurman Signature Cut diamond in the white gold setting with the diagonally set cabled bands. "To represent the two hearts joining as one," he'd recited. He was right.

"Good, you remember it," Jake said, taking in my expression and angling the inside of the band toward me so I could see it. "One minor alteration."

There on the flat inner surface of one band engraved in a thin delicate script were the words *Charlotte & Jacob Logan,* and on the other band in the same elegant hand, *Kassiwi passego.*

That melted my heart all over again. "How'd you…" I began, looking up at him with tears forming in my eyes.

He winked at me. "I know you, Charlie." He slid the ring on my finger and pressed my hand to his lips, whispering, "Kassiwi passego."

"Kassiwi passego," I nodded. Grinning, I twined his fingers in mine and put a finger to my mouth, dragging him across the room. He cocked his head in wonder as I reached for the handle and quickly yanked the door open.

Charlene tumbled in falling to the floor with Marcus landing in an equally unceremonious heap atop her. Jake barked a laugh and shook his head at the sight of the two being caught eavesdropping.

"How'd you…" he started, still laughing as Marcus tried to help Char up.

I sighed. "I know Char."

"Well, you two weren't talking loud enough," Char pouted then her eyes drew a bead on my hand. "Ohmygod!" she exclaimed, then rushed me with a big hug, toppling us both to the carpet with her enthusiasm. We giggled helplessly as Marcus and Jake looked on smiling.

"Congratulations, man," Marcus said, clapping Jake on the back. "I know you'll be very happy together."

"Thanks… for everything, Mark," Jake replied, still watching Char and I on the floor. She had me pinned down, straddling my legs as she gripped my hand in hers to examine the ring, one eye closed, the other glued to the jewelry.

Satisfied with the inspection Char angled her head over her shoulder to peer at the two men. "Welcome to the family, Jake! Does this mean you forgive me, too?"

I dumped Char off my lap, both of us sitting on the floor staring up at him expectantly. In my excitement I hadn't even considered that he might not exactly harbor any happy feelings for Char, given that she'd started this mess.

He frowned at her, thinking it over, then pulled Char up off the ground holding both her hands in his. "How could I *not* forgive you, Char? If it wasn't for you none of this would have ever happened, and I wouldn't have met Charlie. But," he warned, "There's one condition." She waited patiently, searching his face for his response. "You never, and I mean *never*, ask her to switch again, okay?"

"Promise," she beamed, nodding frantically as she threw her arms around him and kissed his cheek. He hugged her in return, and I'd never been so happy to see another woman clinging to my man. No, not just my man. My *fiancé*.

Hmm. My fiancé. That has a nice ring to it don'tcha think?

Marcus helped me from the floor and drew me into a hug. "Take care of my boy, all right?"

I nodded, smiling. "And you be good to my sister."

"Of course."

Jake cleared his throat. "A-hem." We both angled to look at him, Marcus's arm still around my shoulder. "Maybe one last switch."

We all laughed as Char and I traded positions.

"How can you tell 'em apart, J?" Marcus asked sliding his arm around Char's waist. "If you two were dressed the same I'd be screwed."

"Different shades of gray," Jake whispered, nuzzling me tightly from behind.

Marcus grumbled, "Get a room."

"Since all is right with the world again, can we eat now?" Char asked, pressing a hand to her belly. "I'm starving. And I'm sure if we all ask really nicely sweets'll whip us up something delicious."

Jake groaned behind me. "Oh, god! Can I get that ring back? I forgot you can't cook!"

I lightly elbowed him in the ribs and turned to slap his arm.

"What do you mean? Charlie's a great cook. You didn't like the crab canellonies?" Char asked, genuinely confused.

Jake smothered a laugh and I slapped his other arm.

"Such a violent woman," he joked, his chuckle turning into a rumbling laugh as he deflected my playful assault. "Things got kinda sticky after the chocolate tarts! Which reminds me, angel-face…"

I instantly recognized the glazed look in his dark brown eyes. "Oh, no." I shook my head, backing away from him slowly. "You gotta feed me first, Logan."

"Fine," he griped, taking a step toward me and gathering me again in his arms. "Food first, then a shower?"

I bobbed my head, remembering we'd had the same conversation the first day in the gym. "Y'know, baby, I think this time I'll take you up on that."

Epilogue
{8 months later}

"Ladies and gentlemen, for the first time, Mr. and Mrs. Jacob Logan," the DJ announced as Charlie and Jake entered the grand ballroom. A thunderous applause went up and people whistled and cheered as the married couple strode to the center of the parquet floor.

Jake bowed slightly as he took Charlie's hand; a beautiful song she had chosen but didn't care about right now began to play. All she was focused on was her husband.

"Hey, angel-face," he said, drawing her close as they moved on the dance floor.

"Hey yourself, Logan," she replied smiling up into his deep brown eyes as her arms went around his neck. "I can't believe this is happening."

"Really?" he asked, pressing his mouth to her ear. "You're the one who planned all this. I was just along for the ride."

"You sound just like your father," she said.

"Well, he gave me some very good advice. He said," Jake began, before mimicking his father's voice, "'Son, if you wanna get through this alive, just smile and nod.' Before I knew it, we were already at the 'I dos'! So I guess I'm stuck with you now."

"A chip off the old block," she said dryly. "And for the record, Char, Amanda, and your mom planned all this. I was perfectly content to go to the courthouse months ago."

"And you'd have been widowed *before* the 'I dos'! Mom would have killed me if I robbed her of a full-blown wedding with all the trimmings," he chuckled. "You're the daughter she never had, and I'm her only child. Don't know about you, but I only plan on doing this once."

"Yeah, you'd better," she warned with a grin, resting her chin on his shoulder before adding thoughtfully, "Although I did hear *Free Money*'s recasting."

Jake stopped dancing to look at her, seeing she was struggling to keep a straight face. "Not funny," he grumbled as she broke into a laugh.

As they went around the dance floor Charlie caught the smiling eyes of a dear friend. Amanda, one of her bridesmaids, was chatting with her new beau Scott, who had actually become pretty close friends with Jake after all the drama had been ironed out. Whenever they were all free, Charlie recruited Jake, Marcus, and Scott to help restore the Harley while Char and Amanda went shopping. She had joined them on only one occasion and immediately regretted it when they entered their sixth hour of shoe shopping with no immediate end in sight.

Nonetheless, the mansion she and Jake had purchased was fully decorated thanks to the two shopaholics and her new mom, Nathalie, and Anthony—dad—had customized their expansive garage with help from Jake who had a yen for collecting vintage cars. She looked forward to cookouts on the patio with all of their friends and family, movie nights curled up in the theatre room, and quiet moments alone with Jake on their boat.

And kids! According to Jake's mom, "Lots and lots of them." Jake happily told Charlie that meant, "Practice. Lots and lots of it!"

She looked forward to that, too.

It was hard to believe that only an hour ago hundreds of guests—which was the '*revised* revised short-list'—had attended the ceremony and were now joining them for the reception at the event the tabloids had considered the first of the two "it" weddings of the year. Of course, this was after months of front-page snapshots of the couple spotted leaving a club or out eating, with cheesy titles like DOCTOR LOVES DANGER and BEAUTY AND THE BADBOY. There had even been a picture of a tearful Tamara, the caption lamenting, "She stole my fiancé!"

Work had been difficult at first. Once patients started to recognize who she was some would ask her personal questions in spite of the fact that they were losing blood at the time. Although the show had never aired, there was enough info on the internet to give the curious researcher fodder for the gossip fire. But through it all, the love she and Jake shared grew stronger and deeper. An overwhelming feeling of peace enveloped her, and, as if sensing her emotions, Jake squeezed her tighter.

"You know a lot of folks, baby," Charlie marveled, watching the clusters of people observing them as they went around the dance floor.

"Says the woman who is currently the most recognizable ER doc in the world," he retorted. "You could have let the Style Channel make this into a TV special, sent fewer invites, and saved a few trees."

Charlie shook her head. "No way was I gonna let this be televised. I'm *beyond* through with being a reality-TV star," she said, thinking about the number of security guards that had been hired to keep the press away today. They'd only had one incident leaving the church and getting to the secret location of the reception. A bold photog had jumped onto the side of their truck, camera flashing uselessly against the dark tinted windows.

"Good. Except you'll be doing this all over again in five months," Jake reminded, spinning Charlie away then pulling her back as the crowd *oohed* and *aahed*.

Charlie's eyes found Char and Marcus—the maid of honor and the best man—who were cuddled on a seat together near the dance floor, smiling at them. In five short months they'd all be in Costa Rica for the Broussard wedding where the roles would be reversed. She imagined their wedding would be as highly publicized as this one was; every magazine and show asking for an exclusive or trying to get pictures. She sighed theatrically. "The downside of marrying the rich and famous."

"Oh, yeah? So what's the upside? Apart from the sex, of course?" Jake grinned slyly, "And while I'm thinking about it let's speed this whole reception thing up. I can't wait to get you out of that dress."

"Hmm… apart from the sex? VIP access to the Red Room, of course," she scoffed, leaning back a bit so he could see her sardonic frown. "Why else do you think I married you, Logan?"

Jake threw his head back and laughed. "Is this what it's gonna be like for the rest of our lives?"

"Absolutely!" she exclaimed as the song came to an end. The sound of silverware clinking against glasses filled the room as the crowd called for the newlyweds to kiss. "Think you can keep up with me for a lifetime, Logan?" she challenged with a grin.

Jake thought about everything that had brought them to this moment; the audition, the show, the confusion, and the reconnection. Never had he imagined finding a woman he could love so much then, and was overjoyed to find he loved her even more now. He kissed her passionately as if they were the only two people in the room. The guests whistled and cheered, and when they parted he touched his forehead to hers, staring lovingly into his wife's glowing gray eyes. "Oh yeah, angel-face. I'm looking forward to it."

ABOUT SABLE JORDAN

What's to know about Sable Jordan? Hmm. I'm a tough tomboy type with a hidden romantic streak. I love to read, especially romances, romantic thrillers, romantica, and suspense stories laced with romance. See a theme here? I started writing when I was a child, but put it aside for other endeavors—it's my Sagittarian nature, always aiming at every shooting star. Once I got old enough to understand how to balance my time and energies (yes, that's code for "operate on less sleep"), I went back to writing. At first it was just catharsis with little intent to publish, but I figured I'd let someone other than my mom read it. (Hi mom!)

I don't always write according to the formula. I figure however it comes out is how the story should be told. And even though I've got room, I do most of my writing in the closet. Weird? Maybe. I'd never claim to be "normal". I find myself spacing out at inopportune moments because I'm working a scene out in my head.

Aside from that, I hold a degree in biology from UC Berkeley and I'm a certified massage therapist. I have a wicked sense of humor, I love dogs (especially pit bulls, they're so misunderstood), every variety of music, and candy… lots and lots of candy. Candy is my kryptonite, but I think all the sugar helps me make the love scenes so sweet!

To find out more about my work you can visit my site www.sablejordan.com. And I love to hear from fans (and critics, if slightly less so) at sablejordan@yahoo.com.